Renegade in the Hills

by Andy Thomson

Bob Jones University Press, Greenville, South Carolina 29614

Renegade in the Hills

Edited by Rebecca S. Moore
Cover and illustrations by Stephanie True

Greenville, South Carolina 29614

ISBN 0-089084-494-1

Printed in the United States of America

20 19 18 17 16 15 14 13 12 11 10 9 8

Publisher's Note

Renegade in the Hills is a story about sin on two sides: the drunkenness of a rowdy western outlaw and the legal deceptions of a wealthy cattleman. Josiah Eagle is trapped between the sins of his father and those of a town boss who means to use the law to gain his own ends.

It is tempting to believe that accidents or tragic mishaps occur to God's scheme of things. Young people saved today often come from backgrounds that seem to trap them in the sins of their families or in the sins of the past. The author has written *Renegade in the Hills* in response to a young Christian's complaint that the evils of his deceased father continued after him. But, as Josiah Eagle learns, God makes even the wrath of man to praise Him, and He delivers all those who trust in Him.

This is a story about the sovereignty of God working through a young boy's suffering to bring him to salvation. Though it includes a secondary theme about the sinfulness of society at all levels, its primary message is that Christ is able to save anybody in any condition and that He can save to the uttermost.

Dedicated to
Mrs. Marie Bayer

Contents

Chapter 1

Trouble Starts

I was doing a spell at the Boys Home when word came to me that justice was about to get done to my Pa. Vigilante justice. That meant a hanging for sure—no judge, no jury, just a band of angry men with a rope.

Vigilante justice wasn't uncommon. If a sheriff weren't around or if he were crooked, the ranchers would get together themselves and rout out trouble.

Or if trouble came up way outside of town, cowboys would just handle it themselves, under the direction maybe of their bosses.

Word had it that they were going to get Pa at the end of a rope at last—that or burn the place down around his ears. One of the cowboys brought down a quarter of beef to the Boys Home and let me know.

I climbed out the window that night when everyone was asleep and started walking. The moon was out, so it was pretty easy going. I stopped after a few hours and waited until sunup. By then I was hungry, but a fellow's got to do for himself. Not long after light, I hailed a wagon. It was a homesteader bound for the next town. He gave me a ride and two biscuits.

"You're out early," he observed, watching me from the corner of his eye while I ate.

I nodded. "I got business on th'other side of town."

"Young colt like you?"

"My Pa's in trouble."

"Sick?"

"No, he's got some folk mad at him, and I'm gonna try to settle things 'fore someone gets killed."

He gave me a second and longer glance and after a long pause said, "I reckon you're that Josiah Eagle's boy."

I nodded. "The same."

"Don't know that I'd have picked you up if I'd known that right off."

"You got no cause to be afraid of me," I told him. "Or hate me. I'm trying to settle things."

"All the same, blood tells." But then he gave a grunt and didn't throw me off. "Tell me about your old man. He got you right in the thick of things?"

That made me wonder what exactly folks were accusing Pa of—this time. It hadn't troubled me to figure out if Pa deserved lynching or not. I suppose if I'd thought about it I'd have agreed that he did. Pa'd outgambled many a man, and when that didn't work, he could cheat any greenhorn at cards or dice. He'd sold moonshine over his own bar when things got rough and had poisoned about a dozen men by accident (not all at once) on barrel whiskey. He'd outgunned two or three men face to face and five or six from behind. If there was a scheme, Pa would be in on it. If anybody got swindled, you'd know that sooner or later Pa'd be in for a share. But I had stayed out of his affairs.

"Course not," I told the farmer. "He's got no time for a kid. I stay at the Methodist Mission Home for Boys, ten miles back. Been there off and on for two years now. Just outside of the town down there."

"Yeah, I heard of it," he said. "Town of Waterstop. Used to be on the railroad line until the tracks got moved." He chuckled under his breath. "Ain't that just like the railroad? Comes through so folks can build up all their dreams and make a town and then moves the tracks over twenty miles."

I didn't like the way he said it. I got the idea that I'd hooked up with some bitter, greedy farmer who was grudging the good life. I wished I hadn't spoken up so freely about my business.

Almost like I'd predicted my own troubles, he asked, "What would your Pa pay for a nice safe layover until the trouble up yonder at Willow Creek blows over?"

Pa lived in a tumble-down old shack way out of town near the hills where he could make an escape if he needed to. He hadn't done any work on it, but the fact was that he had a homesteading claim on the place. Somehow every year he managed to fake things to the land agents to make it appear that he was improving the place.

That—like as not—was the main reason the vigilantes had decided to rout him out. Pa had picked out a mighty nice stretch of grazing ground for himself, and he'd fenced it in. The homestead lay in a shallow dish of land, and it caught a lot of rainwater off the mountains. It was prime for cattle, but he'd run only about fifty head on the whole hundred acres, and even that was just for show, because they weren't much cared for. Pa was ornery as they came and likely had done it just to spite the big cattlemen.

I glanced at the homesteader. "Pa ain't never paid for nothing 'cept groceries now and then. What he wants he either wins or swindles or gets with a gun."

"He might think twice with all the talk of lynching I'm hearing."

So it *was* that bad. This poor old dirt farmer had heard of troubles kicking up too. If news had spread that far, then I sure didn't have much time.

"Who told you 'bout lynching?" I asked.

He just shook his head. "Let's talk money first."

"I don't have any money," I said—which was true.

"Your Pa's got plenty from what I hear. Now you speak up—what'll he pay to save his worthless life?"

"Mister, I told you true. Pa gets mighty offended when folks expect him to pay for things. And I don't dare speak up for him—not about anything. You come 'long with me if you want and try to work out a deal. But I can tell you right now: he'll either laugh you out of that shack or shoot you."

Next thing I know, the old coot goes and draws a Navy revolver out of his belt and points it at me. "Not if I got his kid hostage."

"Hey," I said. "You got my old man figured all wrong. He'll shoot you right through my body. He don't care."

"You take the reins and keep your mouth shut," he said.

I took the reins and shut my mouth. This was the third time in my life I'd sallied out to save Pa's hide, and each time it got more and more dangerous. This was the last time, I promised myself. What I'd said to this two-bit broken-down weed grubber was true enough.

Pa'd shoot him right through me if he felt like it. I was good enough for Pa when Pa felt like braggin' to somebody or when he got to feelin' guilty about how rotten he was, but if it came down to my life or Pa's, Pa was going to save himself.

We drove on in a long silence. It was near twenty miles to Willow Creek, so we were going to be on the road until late afternoon. I got to thinking about this fellow.

A homesteader might just pack his rifle along on a long trek to town, but handguns weren't the style for farmers. Most cowpunchers used a handgun in a holster to be handy with slugging wolves or coyotes at night. But a farmer pestered by varmints would just take out his rifle and walk his fences. When a farmer carried a handgun, that generally meant he was hunting humans. When a farmer rode nigh onto twenty or thirty miles into town toting a handgun, that meant he was going where trouble was brewing. The truth hit me all at once. This old dirt farmer had been packing that gun to join in with the vigilantes.

Chapter 2

A Smell of Money

"You want me to go 'round the town to Pa's?" I asked him as we neared Willow Creek. "Or drive through town?"

"Go 'round," he said. "We'll need to get a jump on the mob. I don't want to tip them off."

"You'd be a lot safer showing up with the mob," I told him.

"Your Pa's no fool. He'd just as soon split his cache with me and ride out alive as have that fool mob get it all and leave him hung from a barn rafter."

So that was the trick. Somehow this pack of fools had got the idea that Pa had a lot of money stashed away on the homestead, and they were reckoning on splitting it once they'd lynched him.

Well, Pa had been too handy with poker and drinking and other things to save up much money. Every now and then rumors did fly around that he was sitting on a fortune out there, but this was the first time the rumor had taken fire.

"Look, mister," I said. "I know Pa, and he never was one to hold onto money. If you're looking for a fortune, you're looking in the wrong place. The only thing you're gonna find out there is hot lead."

"He's taught you good, ain't he?"

I grimaced. "The only thing my old man ever taught me was to stay out of his way. And I wish I'd learned my lesson."

"Whatever happened to your Ma?"

"I don't know."

"Folks say you and him harked out of Tennessee."

"I don't know that either. Far back as I can remember is living with some half-breed Indians up in the hills. They were all renegades. That's where Pa took up his last name of Eagle."

"What happened to them?" he asked.

"Some got shot; some got pneumonia and died—they can't recover from white man's diseases—and the rest just split up."

"You been raised a reg'lar outlaw, just like folks say," he told me. "And they're gunnin' for you too."

I looked at him. "What?"

"You heard me. Keep drivin'."

"They're fixing to lynch me?" I asked. "What'd I do?"

"Your name's Josiah Eagle, just like your Pa's; I guess that's enough," he said. "Guilt by 'sociation," he added.

"That cowpoke who rode down to the Home yesterday didn't say nothing 'bout me being in danger," I said.

"Does that cowpoke happen to be one of Bart Gibson's men?" the farmer asked. "Gibson's got it in bad for you and your Pa. I think you better pick your friends more careful from now on, boy. They was intent on lurin' you into a box trap."

"But what'd I do?" I asked. "I been way over at the Home all this time."

"Maybe that's so and maybe not, but folks in town are sayin' that you been helpin' your Pa in his lawless ways, including stealing cattle and holding up cowpokes on the road. The minute you'd 'a' set foot in that town, you'd 'a' been strung up too." He waved the muzzle of the gun at me. "So you jest thank your lucky stars I found you first."

It's true I was only fourteen, but there'd been some outlaws hung or horsewhipped that were only my age. Fourteen was plenty old enough to do a man's work either inside or outside the law in those days, and you got paid the same wages.

I could understand why Gibson had it in so bad for Pa. Pa's land got right in the way of Gibson's grazing territory. Gibson was a big rancher. But why he'd go for me was more than I could figure.

"Well, I reckon you have saved my life," I told the farmer.

The afternoon sun was on the wane by this time. I steered the horses off the road and onto a narrow wagon track that would take us around to the homestead, out of sight of the town. I had to get rid of this dirt farmer. True enough, he'd likely saved my life, but it sure wasn't out of brotherly love. And likely enough we were both going to get plugged by my Pa.

We were right near the creek, where the ground got steep and choppy. The horses had to put their shoulders to it to get the wagon up a rise in the ground. I started whipping them up with the reins. “Ya! Ya! Git on, you old nags! Git on!”

“Hey, steady,” the farmer said. “Don’t treat them horses so, you fool.”

“What’s takin’ them so long?” I asked. “Git on you sorry nags, git on!” I beat them hard a few more times and pulled the reins back tighter in my left fist.

He was plumb distracted from his gun. “You crazy fool! Leave off them horses!”

He was watching the near horse as it arched its head back, and just as quick I slapped the ends of the reins right across his eyes. Twice.

He covered his face with his free hand, and I jumped up and grabbed the gun with my right hand, pushing it away from my chest, and I used my other hand to give him a hard box right across the opening of his ear. It was an Indian trick, and a right effective one too. He yelled in pain and fell right out of the wagon. I jumped out too. I had the gun.

The horses had spooked a little at the commotion, but they’d been too intent on getting up the steep hill. I reined them in and set the brake, keeping him covered the whole time.

“Look up,” I said to him. “I know you’re awake. Keep your hands where I can see them.”

“What’d you do to my ear?” he asked. He’d rolled onto his back and lay looking up at me like a rattler with a broken back.

“Just pushed a little air into it and pulled it out right fast,” I said. “It’ll feel better in a few days.”

I had a knife on me, and I cut the traces on the horse nearest me.

“Hey, what’re you doing?” he asked.

"Saving your life and mine, I hope," I told him as I set the horse loose. I cut the other one free and swung astride it. He came up while I was getting onto it, but I covered him with the gun. "You just walk on to town," I said. "Shouldn't take you more than an hour. I ain't gonna keep this horse very long, so you might get it back."

"You're dead," he told me. "And so's your Pa."

"We'll see," I said. "But I'm telling you true when I say I ain't never helped him in nothing. That lynch mob you're fixing to join ain't after justice—it's after money. But there ain't no money out there. Adios, friend."

Chapter 3

Pa

I was so mad at Pa and at the world when I rode up to the homestead that I wasn't careful at all how I came into the place. I just kicked open the front door and walked in.

He was setting on a stool in the front room and he swung his shotgun around onto me so fast that I thought for sure I was a goner. I didn't think anybody could stop a shot that he'd been so bent on making, but Pa did stop it. For a split second we just stared at each other, and then he said, "You're a tomfool to walk in here like that. Git out of here!"

"There's a mob coming after you," I told him.

"Go on now, tell me something I don't know," he said with a sneer.

I realized that he already knew they were coming. That was why he'd been covering the door.

Pa was balding and had a furry brown beard. He was wearing his usual wool pants and long johns underneath and a long-sleeved undershirt with his old suspenders. The whole front room of the shack reeked of wood smoke and whiskey.

"They think you got money out here," I said, "and I reckon that after they do you in they're thinkin' of splitting it up. Old Man Gibson's heading it up, from what I figure."

Pa gave a slight incline of his head. "Well, you got brains, all right," he said. That was the first compliment he'd ever paid me, I thought—anyway as far as I could remember.

"And they're fixing on stringing me up right along with you," I said. "So I'm gettin' out of here right now. I don't look for any gunfighting."

"Goin' back to those old wimmin at the Home?" he called as I turned my back on him.

"You bet I am," I said.

"No you ain't." And I heard the hammers on the shotgun click back.

I opened the front door and turned to look at him. "Go on, shoot," I said. "I don't care. I'm tired of risking my skin for you. You just shoot and give them vigilantes a reason to string you up."

He jumped up. "Now look, Son; you go out on that there road, and you'll be bait for the birds, you hear me?" He set down the shotgun.

That was the first time he'd called me son too. I glanced back at him.

"Them boys ain't gonna let you git back to that Home," he told me. "They mean to get you and me both in this here shack, and if they got to force you back here at gun point, they'll do it."

I shut the door and turned around to look at him.

"How come?" I asked.

He took his seat again. "Don't be a fool. You been using your head—use it some more. If those tomfools out there think I got money and a claim to this here land, then they got to get rid of me and my heir. So Gibson cooks up a story that you're my 'complice. And he gets some of his men to swear on a Bible that they been held up by you and me both."

"I got an alibi—" I began.

"He'll make sure you never get to court, boy," Pa told me. "He wants the money that he thinks is here, and he wants this here homestead. Gibson's run his wheels over better folks than us. You ain't nothin' but a cuss raised by Injuns to him."

"You plannin' on just sittin' here and having a gunfight with forty men?" I asked him.

"I was meanin' to head into the hills," he told me. "But I thought you might be 'long to warn me. Didn't think it p'lite to leave you here to face them."

I thought he was saying it rude—sarcastic—like Pa always talked to me, but he had a strange look in his eyes. He glanced out the crack in the shutters as though keeping watch.

"Well let's get going, " I said.

"You run 'long first," he told me. "There's a horse saddled up with a pack of pork and bread on his back. You git up near the caves and wait for me. It'll take weeks for those chuckleheads to find us there."

"What're you gonna do?" I asked him.

"Stay behind and fire this place over their heads if I can."

"Pa—" I began.

"Don't you stand there and tell me how to fight, boy!" he yelled. "I'll cut you down to size pretty quick! You blockheaded idiot!" Then as though to himself he added, "Gimme peace from striplings who can read and think it makes them smarter than their betters. You git on your way, you mission-home woman, and leave the fighting to a man!"

"Well you just stay and git shot!" I yelled back. "I'm mighty tired of gettin' caught in wars of yours. You better be glad this mission-home woman likes that mission!" I swung open the door. "'Cause when I git back there outta these hills, I ain't ever comin' after you agin! This's the last time I risk my skin for you, old man! I'm mighty tired of lookin' down the barrel of a gun for the likes of you!"

I went out and pulled the door shut as hard as I could, but you just can't slam a door on leather hinges.

I trotted out to the barn and got the horse that Pa had left saddled, and I swung up on him.

Sunset was coming, and the vigilantes would be showing up soon by torchlight. This was the first time Pa'd ever made any provision for me like this, getting a horse ready and planning to have me join him.

As I trotted the horse past the back of the house, I had half a mind to yell that I didn't mean it or to yell something that would make it end as kind of a joke now that we'd both spoke our pieces.

But then I figured that he'd done all that to make me an outlaw with him. I never had been his accomplice, but now that we'd be holed up in the hills for a few months, I could see that he was just planning on it. Josiah Eagle and Josiah Eagle, outlaws.

"I'm skippin' out first chance I get," I promised myself. "He's not makin' me an outlaw."

Chapter 4

Pa's Secret

I rode hard up into the hills while the twilight grew. The land passed quickly from rolling to jagged. I still had the revolver I'd snagged from that dirt farmer, and I kept it handy in my belt. I was half-expecting vigilantes to be holed up waiting for us.

But they must have supposed that Pa'd be caught napping. Nobody tried to stop me. Still, I figured that once that dirt farmer got into town and told his story, they'd try to cut off Pa's escape. He'd better get out in time.

All the same, Pa'd worked himself out of some pretty tight squeezes in his lifetime. Gibson could match him for nastiness, maybe, but not for brains.

After a while I had to lead the horse on foot. In some places the bedrock gave way to trees. I didn't mean to take the horse all the way up, so I tethered him in a stand of trees and toted up a bedroll and a load of grub.

The light wasn't good and the trail got narrow and scary. I toiled up the mountain for maybe an hour and a half before I groped my way into the place Pa called his secret camp. It was nothing more than a dug-out hollow in the ground, hidden from below and on either side. The rock around it formed a kind of rim, and someone passing by would never guess there was a sunken piece of land there. Trees came up close in a half circle around it.

I waited for the moon to rise and then went down and brought up the last load. By then midnight was well past, and I kept expecting Pa.

There were ledges and cliffs that you could shinny out on to get a look at the countryside, and I knew of a place where I could get a sight of the homestead. If he'd fired it, I'd be sure to see it.

I cut the horse loose and let it go. After that I made my way along the mountain until I came to my lookout point. There didn't seem to be anybody nearby, but I waited a bit to be sure. I wasn't about to make myself a target if anybody was up there hunting for me.

From the lookout I saw fire down below, and I judged it to be the homestead and barn going to coals. They must have been fired hours earlier. So where was Pa?

I didn't stay long on the lookout point. If they'd got Pa, they'd be coming after me. And if they hadn't got Pa, and he caught me away from the camp, he'd skin me alive. I started back up to his hiding place.

It was quiet up there. Quiet and cold. Night in the mountains can be a fearsome thing in the late summer. I wrapped a blanket round myself and longed for a fire, but I didn't dare light one yet. If he was being chased, a fire would bring folks like a beacon light. I thought maybe a low fire wouldn't be spotted from ten feet away, owing to the cover in the secret camp. But the night was still, and a fire could be smelled.

I must have dozed off about four or so, and when I opened my eyes, my feet were numb in my boots, and there were things rustling round in the trees. No Pa. The sun had come up.

I scouted around and didn't sight anyone. Way far down there were boot prints and signs of horses. Somebody had come up to look around, but they'd missed me by more than a mile.

I scrambled back up to the secret camp. Nearly a whole day had gone by since I'd eaten anything. It was nigh onto ten o'clock, so I made a low fire and went into the sacks to see what he'd set aside for us. At sight of the first sack I almost yelled in surprise. It was all money.

"Pa!" I heard myself exclaim. I was that shocked. After that I kept quiet while I poked through the sack. It was all kinds of money—Federal notes and old Confederate bills and Mexican paper money and lots of different coins—twenty dollar gold pieces being the most common. The bills were all neatly stacked and wrapped with paper wrappers, but the coins were in a mishmash in the bottom. I rummaged through the rest of the gear he'd packed on that horse. There was another sack full of money too. The third sack—and I was glad, because you can't eat money—had pork and flour and such.

I made myself a meal and thought about what to do. I tied up all the sacks and made them into a pack with the bedroll, and that was when I noticed the first odd thing. There was only one bedroll. In fact, there'd been only one tin cup and one plate and one knife.

But Pa had said he'd planned on me to come. Then I thought that maybe he'd been thinking to tote up his own bedroll and gear, but that was ridiculous. Pa had known he'd have to go light if he'd been planning on firing the house over their heads.

Then I reasoned that maybe my coming had been a big surprise to him after all, but he'd acted like he'd been planning on it so he wouldn't look stupid. But that didn't make sense either, because if I'd been just an extra mouth to feed and an extra body to keep warm, he'd have let me take off on my own instead of threatening to shoot me if I did.

No, he'd been planning on my coming all right. That was the reason he hadn't shot me through the door like he would have done if he'd been expecting only trouble.

Then it struck me that Pa'd probably had his own plans as to where he was going to hide out. But then why leave all the money with me? Pa wasn't exactly a trustful man, and there'd never been more'n a spoonful of trust between the two of us. I'd burn the money for spite, and he knew it.

Well, whatever his plans, I had to get the money out of the way where it couldn't slow us down. I'd take it up to the cave and store it there.

Chapter 5

The Cave

I knew the mountains and hills around Willow Creek like I knew the ground between our shack and the barn. Before I'd gone to live in the Boys Home, I'd roamed around the hills plenty just to keep out of Pa's way.

Finding the Home had been a piece of luck for me. You only got a beating if you were found out, and even then it was by some old woman or old man who used a hickory switch. Pa'd been mighty fond of the buckle end of his belt, and he'd generally let me have it whenever he felt like it.

The Methodist Mission Home for Boys was for God-fearing young men, so I instantly became one. I learned all the rules and followed them, and I kept my mouth shut unless I was spoken to, and then I always added a *ma'am* or *sir* to what I said. And since they taught me to read there, I took to reading anything they had on the place, and that way I stayed out of trouble with the other boys.

The place was run by a little old spinster woman, her sister, the sister's husband, and a widower who'd been to some place called the mission field. I'd figured it was some place on the high seas because they were always talking about lost souls and throwing ropes to their sinking fellow men and all that. Besides, it sounded far away.

But a paper came every now and then to the Home. It was called *Youth's Companion,* and it was that paper that first set me straight about the mission field. Finding out what the mission field really was showed me what a good thing it was to keep my mouth shut. That paper had lots of stories in it too. All the boys liked to read it, and I guess that having to miss out on a reading of the *Youth's Companion* was about the worst punishment for any of us. I always read it all the way through from front to back because it helped me find out how a God-fearing boy of the Methodist persuasion was supposed to act.

But now what were they going to say when they found out I'd run away? Oh, I'd told Sister Erlis all about Pa and had painted it up good and sad for her. She'd figure I had run off to him. And Brother and Sister Hampton and Brother Clarke had all heard something about Pa from neighboring folks. Surely they would hear that he'd been burned out and run down. And if they got wind of the stories that were going around about me, they'd likely speak up publicly and say I hadn't been out robbing people.

But in the meantime, I needed to hide out, and I needed to find out what Pa's plan was and where he'd gone.

Pa knew the cave as well as I knew the mountains, but I wasn't so lucky. I didn't like caves, and I knew that this one had a few different entrances and one big drop-off somewhere inside it.

I packed up the sacks of money and toted them up above the camp and into the cave's mouth. It was just a tiny hole alongside a big rock, and you'd likely miss it except for the draft blowing out of it. I had to get down on my belly and slither in for a few feet, but then it widened up. I crawled on hands and knees as far as I could see by daylight.

This wasn't what you'd call a real popular place—not like some caves where folks go exploring and have picnics and all that. This cave was set high and out of the way. Pa had stored a lantern and a box of matches under a lean-to made of three flat stones. The matches were still good, and after some trouble because of the draft, I got the lantern lit.

But even with a light, the cave spooked me plenty. Dark and big. I'd been in it once or twice before with Pa, and I hadn't liked it then either, although I knew with Pa never to act like anything scared me.

Down lower, on another level of the cave, there was a stream that flowed through, but up here it was dry and quiet. You could see that the place had been all hollowed out by water—maybe by the waters of Noah's Flood, when the mountains had been covered.

There were huge piles of rock here and there, and I figured those would make good hiding places for the money. I had one or two candles in my pocket, but I left them alone as long as I had the lantern. I went on carefully into the black silence all around me.

At the first big pile of rubble that I found, I worked with my hands, looking for loose rocks to move aside. It was harder than you might think, especially because the rocks were so rough and scratched me, but at last I made a niche for the sacks of money. I put them inside and layered the rocks over them, trying to make it look natural. Then, after lighting one of my candles in the flame of the lantern, I dripped candle wax all over the rocks. I softened up the bottom of the candle and fixed it firm onto the cave wall nearby, where it was smooth. That would be my marker. Anybody who might come exploring would just figure that someone had left a lighted candle on the wall and had let it go out. It was five paces from the candle on the wall to the rocks where I'd hidden the money.

That job done, I went back to the entrance and blew out the lantern. It was still pretty full of oil, but I realized that what was in the lantern was all I had. There would be no refilling it.

Pa had packed us full of money all right, but what good was money when you were holed up in the hills with hardly any supplies and a vigilante mob out for your scalp? I'd have traded it all for some more tools and a few supplies—or better yet, for a new name in a new town.

Chapter 6

I Face the Truth

They'd got him all right. Why hadn't he come with me, I wondered. Why wait for Gibson and the men from town to come and ride you down?

I worked on the camp every day, waiting for Pa to come, but he didn't come, and at last I told myself he wasn't ever going to come again. I was free, but for some reason the taste was mighty bitter.

Something must have told Pa that he'd never ride away from Gibson in the end. He had more brains than Gibson, but Gibson was a man who had more spite. Once the secret was out about all that money, Pa had become a marked man. He'd never get a chance to spend it. He'd never get a chance to do anything. Gibson would always be there waiting to get a crack at him. Gibson had turned the whole town into an army against Pa. They'd despised Pa before, but Gibson had got them hungry for his blood. It's mighty sorry what a mob can do, though I knew better than most how much Pa deserved hanging.

I'd always hated Pa's way of life. I'd always wanted the good things of life—a home, even if it was a poor one, and blood kin, and friends. All my life I'd wanted to be able to read, and I'd wanted to be able to walk down the street of a town like I was any farmer's kid instead of being Josiah Eagle's kid: Josiah Eagle.

And now the town was an army waiting for my blood. They were out to get me, because Gibson didn't want any heirs to the senior Josiah Eagle. I'd have given Gibson all that money if he'd just let me get back to the Home and leave me alone. But there's no dealing with a man of spite. In a way, Gibson was a lot like Pa, but he'd stayed within legal bounds. He wouldn't be able to understand what it was I wanted in the Home, and he wouldn't be able to believe that I wouldn't be out for revenge.

I set up snares to get rabbits, and I cut dry wood with a hand axe. Smoking meat is a tedious job, but I did it many days in a row. There'd been a rifle in the saddle when I'd ridden off, and I'd brought it up to the camp, but I didn't hanker after letting the whole countryside know where I was. So I used snares instead, and I caught rabbits. But rabbits aren't fat meat, and I didn't want to get myself sick eating them, so I pieced out the bacon as much as I could to help them along. There were some greens growing wild that I could eat, and sometimes I went lower to find them. That was when I had my first piece of luck.

I was scrounging around in a stand of stunted pine looking for pine nuts when I felt a breeze on my face and looked up. For a second I didn't see anything special, but then I took a better look. One of the trees had grown all crazy against the crags of the mountain because its roots had been pushed up by the rock beneath. Its boughs and trunk were covering something that was breathing out air and making the needles move. I came up and pushed aside the thick wall of boughs.

It was another entrance to the cave—to the lower level. I went in on my hands and knees. There was a real tight squeeze that almost turned me back when I saw it, but I forced myself through. I had an idea that I was going to need every hiding place I could get.

When I got through the squeeze of boulders, my hands scraped the narrow walls of the cave and felt wood planking. I scrabbled with my fingers against the wood, got a grip on a plank and pulled it away. There was another lantern hidden in there.

Pa had known this place, then. That figured. He was one to know every escape hole in the territory. But when I went farther in, I found candle marks along the cave wall. By that time there was enough room to stand up.

I knew he'd left the cave marks on purpose. I followed them on, with one hand trailing along the wall. After about a hundred paces into a wide room, the candle line stopped. I groped along the wall and shone the lantern on it, looking for another mark somewhere. My boot struck a soft place, and I bent down and felt the ground with my hand. Yes, it was wood covered with dirt. I pulled away more planks and uncovered a treasure worth keeping.

There were wool shirts and pants, a pair of good boots, cans of hardtack, a sack of cornmeal that wasn't mildewed at all, and two smoked bacons, wrapped in cheesecloth. He'd moved all of this out from the homestead, I reckoned, and not too long ago, judging by the newness of the dirt that covered the boards.

So he'd been planning on falling back on this secret cache. I thought maybe there was a chance that he'd had his own plan worked out and I'd still meet up with him, but when I picked up one of the wool shirts, I got another shock.

Pa was a big man and mighty wide. Rawboned and fat, I believe one sheriff had called him. I was rail thin and built out of whipcord. I'd be lost in one of Pa's shirts. But these shirts here were small—cut to my size. The first one I'd picked up was new and store-bought. But the second one I picked up I recognized as one of my old ones that I'd left on the homestead.

There wasn't anything there that was Pa's size. It was all sized for me. He hadn't been planning on sharing the cache with me. It was all for me.

That meant he hadn't planned on meeting me in the hills. He hadn't planned on escaping.

A big lump got into my throat, and I began to cry. But even if he'd been there he'd have told me to shut up. I cried just the same. I didn't know what kind of man Pa was to torment me all my life and then throw his life away so that I could escape. I didn't know what kind of man Pa was, and now he was gone.

Chapter 7

Hide-and-Seek

Pa'd always taught me never to trust fate or providence or whatever was out there ruling things. I used the second cave as a storeroom and didn't leave anything in the camp other than what I'd need for a day or two. I slept light and kept the rifle near me all the time. All the same, I ran into trouble, and it all started with a mountain cat.

He must have been about as dumb as I was, I reckon, to get caught so. I was bumbling through the brush to check one of my snares, and I came up on him all of a sudden—him with his mouth full of my rabbit. We were both so startled that we jumped. I lost my footing and sat down hard, and in my panic I pulled the trigger of the rifle—more or less in the right direction.

That poor varmint had only wanted to escape. But I'd gone and shot him right through the chest, just as he was leaping to get away.

I felt mighty bad for him. Decent folks hated mountain cats—but then decent folks hated me too. And this old boy had just been trying to get by, like I was. I'd have let him take the rabbit if I'd thought about it. But I hadn't thought about it, and now he was dead.

I was way below the secret camp when it happened, but I knew the shot might alert folks if anyone was still looking for me. They'd likely come looking again, and they'd find the cat I'd killed.

There wasn't any way to hide him well. I just skedaddled back up toward the secret camp.

For two days I stayed quiet and kept a strict watch. A hard frost came up on the mountain, and it seemed like I was about to freeze, but I kept up a low fire.

If Pa'd been alive, he'd have kept a stricter watch for a lot longer, but I was already getting sloppy about things. On the third day I came back down to the slopes and nearly got plugged like the mountain cat.

I was walking right open and free across a tumble of rocks, and this slug just smacked into the rock wall above my head and sent rock splinters into my face, cutting me bad.

The sudden pain and the blood half-blinded me, but I didn't wait. I dived headfirst out of the way and snaked on my belly until I got under leafy cover. Then I heard men shouting, and more shots were fired, though they didn't come close.

I had my rifle, but I couldn't see to shoot it, and I didn't hanker after killing anyone. I was still that afraid of being like Pa. I just wanted to get away from them.

I bellied on and pretty soon dropped the rifle. It was slowing me down.

In that hour, a long and terrible game of hide-and-seek was begun. It lasted for the whole rest of the day. My face was so cut up that the blood wouldn't stop, and whoever was looking for me could trail me by that if by nothing else.

I'd lose them for as long as half an hour sometimes, but then I'd hear them again, coming after me.

I finally got back up to the secret camp and went past it, hoping they wouldn't find it. There were more rocks and fewer trees way up there. I began to realize I'd made a mistake to come so high, when I heard them yell and knew they'd found the camp.

That gave me a chance to run through the open up above them, but I think they must have heard me. One of them—and there were at least two—yelled right at me to stop, and another yelled to shoot.

"Don't kill him!" someone said—whether the first man or a third, I didn't know. A gunshot missed me, and I got over a ledge and lost them for a second or two. We raced like that up to the cave. They lost sight of me plenty, but they were close enough to spot me again after just a little chase.

At last I bellied into the cave, grabbed the lantern and matches, and groped my way along in the dark.

I'd vanished right out of their sight, and that must have throwed them for a minute or two, I thought. I lit the lantern and hurried on.

The cave was either a trap or a hiding place. I hoped that maybe they wouldn't have any way of seeing, but it seemed likely that they would have known to have brought candles or something. Not many people knew all of the cave entrances, but just about everybody knew there was a cave up here.

Like I said, caves are just full of heaps of broken-down rock. I climbed over one big pile of it, right near where the money was hidden. As I recalled, there was just a tiny squeeze ahead. I found it and squirmed through. It was a lot longer and a lot tighter than I'd remembered, and just as I got myself wedged into one place, with the lantern pushed ahead of me, I wondered if maybe I'd gone the wrong way and was going to be trapped here.

But just when my nerve failed me, I looked ahead around the glow of the lantern and saw that it got wider farther on. I pushed and got myself loose and went on until I came to a big chamber just filled with broken rock.

By then I had blood from my face all over me, and sweat too, and had been on the run for hours. I couldn't go on.

I scrambled onto the rocks and searched through them. Some were tipped on top of others and could be hoisted around.

I seesawed one huge flat rock up on one end. It was hung just right on the tip of another boulder, and it covered up a fissure among all the boulders below. I eased myself down into the narrow crack and pulled smaller flat stones over me. I blew out the lantern and spit on the wick and then eased that big stone back into place over me. It slid down a little before it got stopped, and in the sliding it ripped part of my sleeve and scraped me good, but I didn't make a sound.

Once covered, I squirmed until I got my head into a safe niche, and I kept my arms up around my neck. I curled up with the lantern between my thighs and that rock heavy on my back and shoulder.

After about ten more minutes, I heard voices, and I knew they were coming. The sweat started to trickle down me. I couldn't see them because of the way I was turned, but light from their candles or lanterns spilled through the fissures all around me.

I felt perfectly visible. But I knew from the Indians that a man won't see things where he isn't expecting them. As long as none of them looked directly into the rocks, they'd likely walk right past me—even right over me.

That was just what happened. There were three of them, and they were either craning to look ahead over the pile of tumble-down rocks, or else they were watching around their boots to get footholds. Two of them went by, but one walked right over me, and the boulder came down hard against my back and shoulders. But I didn't make a sound.

After a while they came back, sounding mighty dispirited. They were grumbling as they came, but one of them spoke up clearly. "Anyway, we can always hope he fell down that pit yonder."

But another one said, "Don't you count on it. Them Eagles are cunning. He's tricked us, but I won't rest until I lay holt of him. The boy's twice the devil his father was."

His father was. Half of me ached at being called anything at all like Pa. The other half ached at hearing it confirmed that Pa was dead.

Chapter 8

First Despair

Some folks might think it odd that I didn't hold it against anybody about Pa. Back then it looked to me like everybody was on one side or another in a kind of big war. Pa and me and the renegades and other outlaws were all on one side, and Gibson and the Home and the town were all on the other side.

And I fully reckoned that our side was the bad side. I didn't want to be on it, but there I was, all the same. I'd known for a long time that sooner or later the other side—the good folks, the homesteading types—was going to get Pa. And even though I figured that Gibson had started it all for his own profit, I still couldn't hate the folks who'd done it.

What I wanted was to get off my side and join the other side. I wanted to be back at the Home, eating regular and learning books and sleeping in a bed. Only now I knew I'd never get there—or if I did, I'd still likely be arrested and then lynched. One sheriff wouldn't be able to hold off a mob. And if that mob was run by Gibson and his hands, they'd take care to find out from me where that money was. And telling them where the money was would be as good as telling them I'd had a hand in stealing it from people.

Pa had died thinking he'd left me his fortune, when all he'd done was leave me in the tightest fix I'd ever seen. I even wondered, while I was lying cooped up in that crack amongst the rocks, if Pa'd done it for spite. But then I figured, no, nor for love either. Pa had produced only two things in his life—me and that money—and he'd stashed us both away in the hills before he made his last stand. We were his spoils of war, his possessions, and he hadn't wanted them folks to get either one of us. It was spite against Gibson that made Pa see me so safe and sound into these hills, not spite against me. As usual, it hadn't occurred to him to think about what I wanted. I don't think it had ever even occurred to Pa that I could want things. Being Pa's son had been about the same as being his mule or his shovel.

At last, when everything had been quiet for a long time, I ventured to move and found that I was stiff and sore. I worked my right hand free and struck a match. There wasn't much room even for a lit match, but the brief and sputtering flame showed me my blood on the rocks below my face. I let the match go out and carefully lifted the big slab of rock off me. It hurt even to straighten up, but the darkness spooked me to hurry and get the lantern lit.

It took a lot of work because my legs were cramped, but I climbed down off the rocks and found the squeeze passage where I'd come in. It took a lot more work to wriggle through it, but I was too gloomy to feel much afraid of being trapped. Somehow it seemed at the moment like a fit and likely ending for me.

But I got through and went on, climbing over rocks here and there and crawling in other places, until at last I came out into the night. I put out the lantern but took it with me. I knew I'd never dare come up to the upper cave again, and I wasn't going to leave anything that I needed behind.

Since they'd found the camp, I avoided it, leaving behind any hope of recovering my skillet or coffeepot or tin stuff. The blanket had probably been slashed up anyway.

I spent the rest of the short night on my way down to the second entrance. That, as far as I knew, was pretty much a secret. Pa had felt good enough about it to use it to stash gear.

I still thought I could stay alive through the winter, but I didn't have any fire left in me. All I could do was wonder what would happen after winter. Was I going to live out my life a renegade in these hills because of money I'd never even wanted?

I kept asking myself why in the world I hadn't stayed safely at the Home without getting messed up in this. Pa would've been killed anyway. I should have known he'd have found out about the vigilantes first. Pa always knew about things before I did. Why did I love Pa when I'd always known he'd never loved me?

Dawn was just throwing down a pink streamer on the mountainside when I got into the second entrance. I squirmed my way inside, lit the lantern, and walked through until I found the stream.

It was icy cold but crystal clear. The blood on my face had dried into a hard mask, and I washed it off. And I cried, not for the first nor the last time since I'd come into those hills.

I got all the blood off my face. The rock chips hadn't damaged my eyes, though my nose was swelled up from where I'd got hit and my right eyelid was puffed out, too, and tender.

I wasn't at all hungry. I just kept climbing and climbing, going on into the cave, leaving little piles of rock wherever I had to choose a passage. At last when I could go no farther, I lay down and put out the lantern and slept like I was dead.

Chapter 9

I Strike Back

I was too scared to go back to the upper camp. Most of my food stores had been stashed safe in the lower cave where I'd decided to live, but I sore missed my gear. Like I said before, I could do for myself, even without the nice things of life like a skillet and a plate. But it was inconvenient.

Soon as I woke up I began searching out a good place in the cave to make my home for the winter. One nice thing about the cave was that it would stay warmer inside than the air outside when winter got bad. I'd learned that the earth itself is an insulator, which is why sod houses are generally easier to get warm than wood houses.

I didn't like living in the dark, but then I knew I'd have to get used to it, and I did, and after only a few days.

There were many passages in the lower level of the cave, and I figured it was possible for a body to get lost if he weren't careful—careful of his direction and careful of his fuel.

I used the lanterns to search me out a good place, and I found one soon enough. I went through and took every right turn—there were two—and squeezed myself through in a couple places and climbed rocks here and there and at last found the stream again.

The stream was going sluggish and slow this time of year. I came over a kind of cliff of big slabs and there it was, like an oasis in the desert, only underground.

It was wide and flat and smooth, and I could see by the light of the lantern that a body could even do with a small rowboat here. I followed it on, walking with the current. The stream narrowed some, farther on, though it was still real placid and calm, like a canal. On either side, the cave floor was smooth as a town home's floor, and real even, though it had a slight slope toward the water.

I could tell plain as day that this place had been smoothed out by the waters themselves. Every spring the waters likely rose and came rushing through here, filling up the whole chamber until the flood season was over. The flood waters had hollowed out the place as nicely as a stone mason could have done.

But I reasoned that if this was where all the flood waters bottlenecked and filled the place, then I was near the outlet of the stream. Sure enough, a little farther on I saw where the stream disappeared into the cave wall.

I shucked my clothes and waded in, leaving the lamp on the stone floor.

It took me a couple of plunges into the icy cold water to find it, but I followed the flow of the water, got under a rock ledge, and came up outside in daylight. It was harder squeezing back in under the rock ledge, holding my breath and all, but I came back up inside the cave.

That was a good enough back door for me. Through the winter at least, this was going to be my new camp. And a good thing too, because I didn't have much oil left to use for hunting anything better.

I'd combined both lamps, but I was about out of light unless I wanted to trust to candles, which were uncertain at best in a cave with a draft.

That was when I got my first notion to strike back.

I sure enough didn't want to make any trouble with the town folks, but I was mad at Gibson and his boys.

While I put on my clothes again, I took to thinking of a way to carry this war to him.

Gibson's cook shack and bunkhouse were a good piece from the town of Willow Creek—even farther than Pa's homestead was. But I reasoned that most of his men had been out combing the hills for me. Winter was coming on, and he likely hadn't laid in his supplies yet.

He'd be sending his boys into town to load up, a task which was likely to take all day. That meant that his foreman and hands would likely pass part of the night at the saloon, getting in their last fling before wintering on the range.

I knew Gibson's brand and his buckboard by sight. I could pick them out from a group.

It was a half-crazy plan, but I was half out of my head with the grief and the pain of all that he'd done to me. I waited for night and then came out onto the mountain. Even if those boys were still out looking for me, they probably were pretty sure I was still holed up, scared out of my mind. They wouldn't be expecting me to come out scouting in the dark.

I was lower now than I'd been in Pa's secret camp, and it didn't take near as long to come out to the wagon road. I walked quietly, and I reasoned that if anyone should come along, I could just lie flat in the grass until he passed. But nobody came. The night was dark: stars, but not much of a moon.

It took me a few hours to get to Willow Creek, and I came in across the tracks and swung around through the houses where folks would likely be indoors and quiet.

The houses were mostly quiet, but up on the main street the saloons were throwing light out onto the dirt street. There weren't any sidewalks. I didn't see any of Gibson's horses, and I could tell that it wasn't a big night in the town—tomorrow was a workday. I'd have to wait for Saturday to come.

That meant finding a hiding place. I took my time choosing out a spot where I could be comfortable and handy to water.

The hotel wasn't much of a place to speak of. It did have a second floor, unlike most of the places, which were only false fronts. But it did have a cellar, and the cellar door was busted. Right outside the cellar door they kept a rain barrel. I decided it was as good a place as any to wait a spell and went down to take a look.

Somebody had thrown some old and busted furniture right down the steps, all in a heap. That was mighty encouraging.

There wasn't much of anything else to see: a lot of old bottles in one corner and some wooden crates here and there. I got some of the crates piled up, and I curled up behind them.

Chapter 10

Willow Creek

I had jerky in my pockets, but all the same, three days seemed a long time in the waiting. A couple times I almost gave it up and went back to the hills, but it rained the second night, so I stayed put. Gibson's men came into town on the third day.

I was sleeping in the cellar by day and roaming around late at night. Willow Creek was a pretty new town. There were three saloons all down at one end of the street, with the livery stable about the middle and the stores up on the other end.

Somebody stayed late to keep a watch in the livery stable on Friday and Saturday nights, but the doors were left thrown open until ten o'clock so that all the late-comers could put up their horses and such without much trouble.

The trick was to strut around like any cowboy and to do it between nine and ten when people were going in and out and not paying much attention.

I went down to the stables about nine-thirty and walked right into a stall with a nice sorrel. We got right well acquainted while two hands came in talking about a streak of luck at poker. I kept the horse mostly facing them while I curried his other side with a brush I found.

They left and I came out again. The stable just wasn't big enough for lots of buckboards and buggies. I reasoned that Gibson's rig would be out back.

I went around the back, and there it was, along with another rig from Getty Coleman's ranch. Coleman was a good rancher who often sent stuff down to the Home, and he didn't always send it by one of his men, either. He came down himself along at Christmas time. Sister Erlis had told me that he was still a bachelor but had come from a big rich family back East. He missed having children around, though why he didn't marry was beyond her reasoning.

When I spied his buckboard, I thought about going to Coleman for help. He'd talked to me a few times back at the Home, and Sister Erlis had even spoken highly to him of my reading and writing and quietness.

But then I recalled the lessons of the last few weeks. I was stuck on the wrong side—a renegade. Coleman had been right good to me in times of peace, but that didn't mean he'd stand by me with Gibson railing at his gates to lay hold of me. Why should Coleman go to fighting over a renegade's kid?

Or more likely he'd take me to the sheriff for the sheriff to protect me, and I knew the sheriff couldn't—not even if he decided to try. If Gibson got his hands all stirred up and then got other folks stirred up, there'd be vigilante justice done. Just like it had been done to my Pa.

I waited by the corner of the back of the livery stable until no one was around, and then I took a look under the cover on Gibson's buckboard. There were all kinds of supplies laid in. I found me a jug of lantern oil and helped myself. He'd also laid in a couple of five-pound sacks of dried raisins. I took one of those and set off.

Chances were Gibson's men wouldn't even notice what I'd taken, and that disappointed me. But I didn't want to go back and tempt fate.

It was powerful awkward trying to haul a jug of oil and a sack of raisins back up to my hide-out, but I got it done at last, though dawn wasn't far off when I came back into the lower cave.

A little mischief had brightened me up some, and I didn't go back to the new camp at the back of the cave to sleep. I stayed by the entrance and ate more jerky and pondered a bit.

Winter was a nice time for a body in a fix such as I was in. Gibson would be getting rid of a lot of the spare men he'd hired for the home site, and some would be off by now if there were any late cattle drives.

Come Saturday night, there likely wouldn't be many folks around the home site at all. I sure didn't mean to hurt anyone, but I figured Gibson owed me a skillet and a coffeepot and a few other things. I decided to pay his cook shack a visit. It would be a long trip, and I planned to go round by the old homestead to look things over one last time.

But it'd be a few days before I needed to leave for Gibson's spread. In the meantime there were snares to set and wood to bring in for the new camp and all kinds of other chores.

First thing I did after a long nap was to divide all my stores and cart half of them way back to the new camp by the stream. Next I hunted out dry branches and brought them back. I got only enough wood to last me a day and a half, and I knew I'd need a good hatchet before winter came on.

Night had come back on by that time. I realized that one problem of living in the cave was that I'd lost all sense of time. There was nothing to go by in there. Whether it had been one day or two days since I'd got back from town stumped me.

I figured after the trip to Gibson's that it wouldn't matter for the rest of the winter whether I knew the days or not. And like as not, if I got to Gibson's a day early, I could hide out in the grasses or someplace until the right time. Doing well in town had made me right confident of myself. Maybe a little too confident.

Meanwhile I hunted out a flat stone to use as a griddle. By that time I'd gone back and forth from campsite to cave entrance several times. Even though I'd restocked on oil, I didn't want to be wasteful, so I tried to get along with my eyes shut a time or two, carrying the lantern. I knew the time would come when I'd have to know the route in the dark, and there's no dark like the darkness of a cave.

Chapter 11

My Second Strike at Gibson

Toward the end of the week I made my way toward Pa's homestead, and it seemed that for once things went my way. Gibson had his men out there, pulling down the fences and rounding up the few cattle that had been Pa's. They'd likely slaughter the branded ones and put their own brand on the others. Whether Gibson had put down money to do such a thing or whether he just considered it spoils of war, I didn't know.

But Pa'd had a right nice group of horses, which I didn't see anywhere. It would have been like Pa to have rounded them up into the barn before he'd fired it, just to make sure that Gibson didn't get them. That's a mighty sorry way for a horse to die, but Pa wouldn't have cared.

Anyway, Gibson's men were camping on the old homestead to get the job done handier, and they had a little wagon loaded with spare leather, picks, hammers, irons, and other tools. In the back of the wagon was their chuck and cooking gear. An old-timer slouched near the back of the wagon, leaned up against the wheel, at work on something.

I'd left the old Navy revolver up in the cave, and I snaked up carefully to the wagon on my belly. The old man at the wagon was mending a bridle. He looked to be at least part Indian, downtrodden and broken, getting the crumbs that Gibson threw him. I took about the biggest chance of my life and in a hoarse whisper called out to him in the language we'd used among the renegades years ago. I don't know what it was—some kind of trade language maybe, or a Blackfoot tongue that lots of them could understand.

Anyway, he jumped, and after a second he glanced furtively the other way and then glanced at me. He gave just a short grunt that meant to come in closer. I trusted him. Men, white or Indian, can deceive, but I'd seen the flicker in his eyes when he'd heard the greeting in a tongue he knew. That old boy knew exactly who I was better than Gibson knew. One word in his language had told him everything—all about being a renegade and getting chased, about seeing the homestead burn around Pa, about pitting myself against Gibson and all his hands. He knew I was Josiah Eagle's boy, Josiah Eagle, and that I needed help, and that I understood his plight just like he understood mine.

I came on the far side of the wagon so that the men out working couldn't see me.

"Take what you need," he said in the soft, mellow language that most white men called gutteral.

"You can come with me, father," I told him. "I have a secret place."

The offer must have surprised him, though the side of his face that I could see didn't show it. "The men hunt you. Take what you need, Josiah Eagle. My days in the hills are over. When spring comes and the hands are busy, come for a horse. I will help you."

I took down a burlap sack and put some gear in it. It took but a second, and I did it as he spoke. Though I knew it was dangerous to linger, I couldn't resist touching his shoulder, just to know he was another human being. There was one person in this world that wasn't my enemy.

I had meant to thank him, but I found I couldn't talk, and even though his face didn't alter, I saw his dark eye squint up some. He'd had a hard life too, I reckon. He pitied me some, and he pitied other folks I didn't know at all. Folks long gone.

After that I crept away and went back to the hills.

I felt bad for that old man, and I thought about him long after I was safe back in my cave. Maybe he'd known my Pa once, or known others who'd known Pa and me, back during our stint in renegade camps. Seemed like the only end for renegades was either an early death at the end of a rope or the endless toil of working in the camps for men who bullied old-timers because they were old and broken.

If I had to be a renegade, I'd take to the hills, but I wanted to be on the good side, and if I ever could be, I'd never treat anybody bad like that. But it was getting to look more and more like all I'd ever be was a renegade: I talked like one, and even though I tried not to, I acted like one and could think like one.

The gear I got was a skillet and coffeepot and a tin plate and a big butcher knife. It was almost piece for piece what Gibson's men had taken from me, except for the big knife. I still didn't have any hatchet.

That meant going far afield to find wood, and the time had come when I'd better load it in. So I organized a system for doing it. I toted in all kinds of wood from outdoors to inside the entrance, pushing it through the first tight squeeze, which was just a short squeeze and not too bad. It was mighty hard in the cave because there were squeeze places to get through, and I couldn't take more than a stick or two through such places. I had to keep going back and forth.

Then when day was done, I got myself through the squeeze and started toting the wood a trip at a time over the first climb of rocks. I left the lantern up on the rocks and blew it out, doing the trips in the dark. I stumbled a couple of times, but I got used to it after a while.

Then I toted the wood from the first climb to the first turnoff, back and forth, back and forth, and in the dark. From the first turnoff I did a stage to the next squeeze, which was high enough to walk upright through, but real narrow. I seemed to spend forever there, going back and forth with just a little bit of wood at a time. Then to the next turnoff, then through a low squeeze place, over some climbs of rock, and at last out to the canal and then down to my campsite. It took me all night to do it, and I slept the day away. Just staying alive was going to take up a lot of my time, but that was good, because it kept my mind off how miserable I was.

Chapter 12

The Beginning of Winter

Winter came at last with a fury. I worked the days away, looking for wood, checking my snares, and smoking meat.

Every now and again I'd spy riders up in the hills, looking for me. They were Gibson's men, on horses marked with the Gibson brand. I had the revolver handy and could have plugged one of them any number of times, but I never did.

A couple of them thought they'd be smart and just camp out until they sighted me. They had a kindling hatchet with them, so I crept in and took it off their gear one night while the one was getting the water and the other was tethering the horses.

They were mostly intent on searching the upper cave for me and hanging around the old camp. They should have seen by the signs that I hadn't touched the old camp since the last time I'd been visited.

But I was a little anxious about them being in the upper cave—not because the money was up there; I didn't think of that—but because there was a drop-off hole in the upper cave that opened into my cave. It was a mighty deep drop—about eighty feet, I reckoned. But if those boys could contrive to come down it, they might just find me out.

The drop-off room in my cave was a few passages and several other chambers over from where I was camping. I had visited it a few times out of curiosity because it was so big. I'd read about cathedrals in some of the books at the Home, and this reminded me of one. Once or twice I'd even tried to pray in there, but it didn't amount to much. We'd prayed regularly at the Home, but it seemed easier to pray when you were dressed in Sunday best with Sister Erlis kneeling by you than when you had on rags and a posse was after you.

And I was starting to feel that being a renegade had barred me from religion. I'd heard heaps about peace and good will to men and such like at the Home, and I'd read all about the martyrs. When Pa'd called the men with religion "women," I didn't pay him no mind. I thought anybody willing to get burned or hung over religion was all man. But I started to feel like I myself had been cut out to be a renegade, and there wasn't any real hope of religion ever getting a hold of me. It had taken a powerful lot of acting to pass off myself as religious at the Home, and it had all come to nothing. Either I just wasn't ever going to really get religion, or there was something in all of it that I was missing.

Anyway, for several days I stayed real quiet and without a light in the cathedral, waiting to see if either of those boys was going to drop in on me. But even though I heard them up above jawing about whether I'd fallen in last time they chased me, neither one of them seemed to have any idea that there was a bunch of passages and rooms down here. It dawned on me that they hadn't figured out who'd taken their hatchet, so one day while they were up above looking for signs of me, I sneaked back to their camp and took one of their bedrolls, on account of them slashing up mine last time.

After that they rode away. I hadn't had me a good laugh since before Pa died, but I sure laughed that day as I watched those boys ride out of the hills with only one bedroll between them. They didn't look too chipper. Maybe it had dawned on them what fools they were or that this time I could have shot them when I pleased, and I hadn't.

I had a hatchet and blankets again and took to cutting wood by day and hauling it back by night. By now I could get through the cave fine without a light—back to my camp anyway—though I carried the lantern with me unlit.

Generally speaking, the cave didn't spook me at all anymore. There were many nights when I had a bright fire going and a dinner cooking of cornbread and rabbit that I'd lean back on the blankets and watch the flames and feel pretty good. I could recall lots of pieces of *The Odyssey* that I'd read at the Home and snatches of stories from the *Youth's Companion,* and these would entertain me again all alone, just like they did when I was there and so happy.

Other times I felt what I was—just one small speck in a big cave in a big mountain, cut off from all the things I'd ever loved: folks' voices and companionship and the dream of having somebody who really cared about Josiah Eagle.

Chapter 13

Midwinter

The ground froze so hard that it'd ring if you hit it. Snow came, and the waters froze. At first a trickle would still get through the cave, but when the streams above froze solid, the trickle became a low, slow pool. It stayed still and looked stagnant. I wasn't short of water anyway, because I could always melt snow.

I got to thinking about bears, because they'll go into caves and curl up for long stretches in cold weather. But there were so many passages and squeezes between me and the cave entrance that I wasn't worried about a bear getting back so far. I was worried about having to get past one if I needed to on my way out. It would take a bear maybe five minutes to widen the tight entrance if he took a notion to do so. So I could expect one to come in and make himself at home at any time, and while he was at it, he'd ruin my secret entrance.

There wasn't anything to do but wait and see, but as time went by, no bears came in for a visit. Either getting into the cave wasn't worthwhile to them or else maybe the entrance was a secret to them the same as to human folks. Or maybe my scent all around the entrance scared them away. Most animals—including wolves—show tail when they get wind of humans. But bears might or might not. They're not used to giving ground. Bears and skunks get mighty pugnacious sometimes.

First I was scared that a bear would come in, but by and by as food got low, I started hoping one might show up. I hadn't anything but the revolver, but I thought if I could get a shot at a bear from cover, I might give him a death wound and trail him till he dropped.

As you can see, I was thinking mighty big for a boy living on rabbits. The bacon ran out, and the cornmeal got low, and rabbits got mighty scarce. If I'd had a rifle, I'd have gone out and looked for bigger game. As it was, I went and hunted again for the rifle I'd left behind weeks ago. I knew that by now it probably wouldn't be any good, but I never did find it.

I had nothing but wool shirts to wear, and I piled them on when I went outside the cave. But the cold was fierce, and I had no gloves. My socks were wearing thin too. I cut back on the food and that made the cold seem even worse when I went outside.

During the autumn I'd spied out gopher holes and such, and I took to digging out varmints and squirrels and clubbing them when I could, but that wasn't too successful. They usually set their nests too far back into their holes for me to reach. And the squirrels were up too high.

I knew there'd be bullfrogs down in the mud under the stream in the cave, but my stomach turned at the thought of eating them. I wasn't starved enough yet to be thankful for bullfrog.

It ran across my mind to snake into town again and forage there, but I'd set myself a stern rule not to steal from innocent folks. Even with Gibson's men I'd only taken back what they took from me. I hated the thought of at last going all out for being a renegade. But I knew I had to make up my mind to steal food while I still had the strength and wits to go down and steal it.

Even so, it would be a lot harder to sneak into town with a blanket of snow blocking out every piece of cover where I'd normally hide. And it was a long walk to try with no coat. At last I decided it would have been hopeless.

My mood turned pretty black, and I was right careless on my trips out. Maybe I thought I didn't care anymore if someone put me out of my misery, but as it turned out, I did.

Just like that mountain cat I had shot way back, I'd come out from one of my snares with my mind fixed on the rabbit I hadn't got, when I found myself covered with a rifle. I'd stumbled right into it, and there was Getty Coleman with a doe over the back of his horse and his rifle on me.

I put up my hands without thinking, and for a second we just looked at each other.

"Well go on," I said at last. "Do it."

"I'd half-thought you'd be dead or gone by now," he said to me.

I just looked at him, and he took in my bare hands, bare head, and ragged clothes.

"How you living, boy?" he asked.

I shook my head.

"I'm not aiming to hurt you," he told me. "Wasn't so long ago I saw you at the Home and thought a lot of you. A real book learner, Sister Erlis said."

It was one of those bad times when I couldn't talk again. I just wondered if he was going to take me back to the town. And if he did, I had to figure out some way to make him shoot me, because I couldn't abide the thought of falling into Gibson's hands at the end of everything. And then I wondered if he'd try to take me back to the Home, but the end would be the same. Sister Erlis didn't have any defense against a posse of Gibson's men.

I started to back away to force his decision. He either had to shoot me or let me go.

"You wait a mite and I'll give you some of this," he said with a jerk of his head at the doe on the back of the horse. That was too much of a temptation, and I stopped.

I stayed where I was, about ten or fifteen paces from him, and he pulled down the doe. He'd already gutted her, and he cut me out a nice big quarter. Then he got the carcass tied up again and back on the horse. He'd kept the rifle by him the whole time, but I don't think he was scared of me. I just stayed still and watched him. But he never looked up to check. He just went on with his work.

He pulled off his gloves and threw them down by the meat on the snow.

"You ain't got no gun?" he asked. He meant a rifle, and I shook my head. He turned the horse around and looked down at me. "You ain't no killer, boy," he said. "I told the sheriff it wasn't true. I spoke up for you to them. I done what I could." It wasn't an apology he was offering me. He just told me what had happened, and I was grateful—later on, I was grateful. At the moment I was just too interested to feel gratitude or fear or anything.

"I'll set this rifle down a piece further, if you'll just set here a spell. It'll help you, I reckon."

I shook my head and at last managed to talk. "No rifle," I whispered. "I ain't a killer."

"Not for food?" he asked me.

But I thought that if Gibson knew I'd gotten another gun, he'd try to make out I was holding up folks. As long as I had food, I'd put off worrying about getting a gun to hunt with. The quarter of venison would see me through a good spell, and maybe by then I'd have got enough small game to get by. I shook my head again.

He stood there with the horse and just looked at me. Later on I realized I must have cut a pretty wild figure. Living alone and hunted had done things to me that I didn't notice until I got around another person. I couldn't talk to him normally. All the emotions from Pa's death to that minute had been bound up like a river in ice, and the sight of a human face had broken up that ice. I had to hold my feelings back, or he'd have thought I'd gone out of my head.

Finally he said, "Josiah, if the Lord would show me how to help you, I would do it. Can you believe that, Son?"

I didn't answer him at all because I didn't know if I believed it or not—if the good Lord was going to mess His hands with Josiah Eagle and if Getty Coleman would obey Him anyway. I didn't know if I'd even like what the two of them decided.

"You come to me whenever you want and I'll help you," he said. "Come secret, because there's men out who'd shoot you. But if you can rest under a man's roof, then you come when you want, boy."

He turned around and walked away, and I put on the gloves he'd left me and dragged the venison back up to my cave.

Chapter 14

Tidings of Comfort and Joy

The doe had been a fat one, and the venison went down good. I ate more that first day than I should have. Not that it made me sick—it didn't. But I knew I was going to have to ration it out.

But I'd been on rations so long that my stomach fought me on my decision. It wanted venison. Even my blood felt like it was calling for more. At last I just ate as much as I wanted and then took to storing it.

Talking to another human being had upset me more than I'd have guessed. I thought about Coleman's voice and his eyes and what he'd done for me, and I cried again. I wanted to go to his spread and get his help, but the other side of me kept telling me that sooner or later Gibson would get me. I trusted Getty Coleman, but I didn't think he could match Gibson in wiles or in spite.

But what I really wanted was just to hear another person talking to me. I wanted to hear another voice. I was so lonely I thought I was going to die from it.

At last I consoled myself that come spring I'd get that horse from the Indian cook at Gibson's and leave.

I'd find a new place and not be a renegade any more. I'd change my name. People would like me.

I kept making myself those promises like a mama shushing her little one, until at last I relaxed enough to fall asleep while the venison smoked above the fire.

I went out and cut wood the next day for smoking more of the venison. The snares were still empty. I started to kick myself for not getting the rifle that Coleman had offered. But in the late afternoon I went down to spy out the place where I'd met him. I knew I ought to make sure he wasn't going to try to trail me, even though I was pretty sure he wouldn't. But when I got near the spot, I saw something hanging from a tree there. I froze and stayed absolutely still for a long time. At first I thought it was a man standing against the tree, but then the wind moved it, and I realized it was a coat.

I stayed stone still because I wanted that coat, but if I'd ever smelled a trap, it was right then. I snaked around and around that clearing like a dog after a scent, but I couldn't spy anyone around or anything else unusual. I waited it out until the sun was on the wane. Shadows from the trees were thrown across the snow, and there was a kind of pink glow on everything before I finally edged up to that coat. It was cut to jacket size and lined with sheep's wool. Right pretty. Wasn't anything in it but two twigs in one pocket. I read the sign right: two days. In two days he'd bring me something more.

I reckoned that the Lord had showed Getty Coleman something. All my renegade sense told me not to show myself to him, but there was part of me more relieved than I could tell. I knew that in two days I would set eyes on somebody not out to hurt me. A friend's a right precious thing, even to a wild renegade boy who only half-knows what friendship means.

Like I said, I'd read the sign aright. Two days later I spied him from cover. He came up and left a parcel for me and then rode away again without a backward look. Coleman wouldn't force himself on anyone, especially someone so scared of being lynched. This time there were cookies and bread in the parcel as well as a note: HUNTERS ON THE MOUNTAIN. SISTER HARFORD TAKES COMFORT TO W. CREEK AT HOMESTEAD. And there was a bundle of seven twigs tied up together.

I knew who Sister Harford was, but the note stumped me. Then I realized it was foolish to stand around in the open. I toted the parcel back up to the camp.

Once safe in the cave I pondered it out. Whatever Coleman was trying to tell me, he had tried to make it clear to me and dark to anyone else.

Sure enough, his warning that there were hunters on the mountain meant that Gibson's hands were watching for me again. Sister Harford was another one of those spinster ladies always looking out for the poor and downtrodden, as the *Youth's Companion* called some folks. I knew she was one to be taking comfort to people, but who W. Creek was, and where his homestead was, and what that had to do with me was too much for me.

I took to eating the cookies, figuring of course that she'd likely fixed them up for Coleman. He didn't seem the kind to bake cookies. Then it started to come to me. If hunters were on the mountain, he couldn't bring me stuff anymore, but he was telling me where to find stuff. Sister Harford would be delivering goods to me. Gibson's men wouldn't suspect a little spinster lady of helping a renegade. But surely she wouldn't come out to the mountain. She was going to W. Creek's homestead.

"Who in this wide world is W. Creek?" I asked out loud. I was anxious to sort it all out, but at the same time I was enjoying myself. Nobody'd spoken to me in months, and the more I spun this riddle out, the more I felt like I was somehow still communicating with Coleman.

The more I ate the cookies, the more I thought that Sister Harford would be a sight better at delivering things to me than Coleman. Those cookies were right tasty.

At last it hit me. W. Creek wasn't a person. It stood for Willow Creek, and right away I knew the place. Down at the foot of the mountain on the other side from Gibson's land, there was an old, deserted homesteader's cabin. It was a far piece from my ranging area but fairly close to the town, and Sister Harford wouldn't raise suspicions if she drove out for such a short spell and came back. She probably was one to be out visiting the sick pretty regularly.

Now the sign read two ways: it could all be a trap. Here I was, getting lured out of my range to an enclosed place. Or maybe Coleman was just trying to help me out because he knew what Gibson was up to. Besides, he had known me from the Home.

But it didn't matter what I thought of the sign. I wanted to go so badly that it was like I didn't have any choice. Coleman had spoken to me and acted kindly toward me. I couldn't refuse the chance to be treated that way again. I was too lonely to turn down the chance of seeing another person.

Chapter 15

Sister Harford

One reason Sister Harford could get by with bringing stuff to a renegade was that she looked so righteous. She had brown hair touched with gray, all done up tight in a bun, and her eyes—though they were blue—were very sober, and she didn't smile much. She even scared me a little bit while I was watching her from cover. Kind of made me feel like I ought to go out and do the polite thing and thank her.

I didn't, because I didn't trust her yet, but she marched right up to the old gutted shack by the creek, and she marched right inside and came out empty-handed. Then she got back into her two-seater, which she drove herself, and marched that horse right out of there. She did it all as though everybody ought to march around leaving packages in broken-down homesteads.

It put me in a sweat to walk into that box trap, but I made myself do it. Wasn't nothing inside but the parcel.

This time it was matches, a bit of bacon, a pair of socks, and a lot more cookies.

She couldn't bring me much at a time because a whole big pack would have attracted too much notice,

I reckon. But as the weeks went by, she kept up the groceries for me. I noticed that she kept her two-seater full of parcels for other folks, too. I was just one on a whole circuit for her.

Somehow even my little bit of contact with her made me more civilized, until at last, watching her go into the shack, I couldn't take it any more. I went in after her.

Just as I got into the doorway, I realized that I'd probably scare her by following her like that, and I real quick skipped aside from the door as she swirled around. That way she'd know she could go. But she turned real fast, and I believe I did startle her, though that's not the kind of thing you ask Sister Harford. If I had startled her, she recovered mighty quick and at once demanded, "Josiah! Can you read?"

The question set me back, but after a second I nodded and said, "Yes ma'am."

With Getty Coleman I'd been all tongue-tied, and I still felt tongue-tied, but Sister Harford didn't believe in being tongue-tied. She asked you a question and just marched an answer out of you, if you know what I mean.

"Can you read well?" she asked.

I nodded. "Yes ma'am."

"Then this is for you."

And she handed me a book. It was my book from the Home—*The Odyssey* by Homer. Books were hard to come by back then, whether you lived in a cave or not. But the Greek classics were among the first bound volumes to get out West, and boys even younger than me had been through English translations of *The Iliad* and *The Odyssey*.

I looked at it a long time and forgot to thank her. I hadn't spoken to a human being for such a long time and had just been given the book I loved best of all, so she didn't tell me to mind my manners. She let it go by.

I looked back at her, and she was standing still, just as composed as you please. If I had scared her at first, she wasn't scared any more. In fact she was looking me over with a kind of look I hadn't ever seen before. Men don't have it. She was thinking I needed a haircut and a bath, and I think she was telling herself that she could do all those things just fine for me. Then she realized I was looking back at her, and she returned my glance. Another thing that made her look so righteous was that she kept her mouth set straight in a line, right prim. It would take me weeks and weeks before I could read past that prim mouth.

"I came in to thank you for all you done for me, Miss Harford," I said. It was a speech I'd rehearsed to myself over several weeks, wondering if I'd ever get the nerve to say it to her.

"Why, you have very nice manners," she said. "And you're a good boy, or so Sister Erlis has told me, so you're welcome."

I sure didn't want her to leave, but I knew I still cut a pretty wild figure, and it might make her nervous if I stayed on. So I walked out ahead of her to make sure everything was safe. But just before I went back toward the trees, she said, "Josiah."

I turned back around to her.

"Getty Coleman can help you," she told me. "If you trust Sister Erlis and the people at the Home, you can trust him. I've known him for years. He'll do what's right."

"Gibson and his men want me dead," I told her. "It ain't a case of whether I'm guilty of a crime or not."

"We know that," she told me.

"The town?" I asked.

"No. Most of the people in the town despised your father and were willing to despise you. But those of us who know of you from the Home—"

I shook my head. "Gibson would ride over all of you, even Coleman."

"Can't you trust in God?" she asked. "Are you going to live forever in the hills?"

It'd been so long since I'd been religious that I didn't answer my usual way. Instead I told the truth. "I was born a renegade. I don't think God will help me. He only helps people like you."

That startled all the primness right out of her. I'd put it over on Sister Erlis pretty well, I suppose.

"Is that what you really believe, Josiah?" she asked me.

I just stared at her, wondering how she could be so shocked at what I'd said. Wasn't I standing here in rags? What did she think had been happening to me all of my life? And now this money and my father's crimes were hanging around my neck. I turned around and walked away from her. Back to the trees and the safety of the cave.

Chapter 16

I Am Found Out

The parcels continued right through the end of winter. Soon it came time for me to think about moving my stuff out of my campsite to higher ground. Once the streams thawed there'd likely be a fierce flood through the cave. And it was time to think about getting away from Willow Creek. I hadn't forgotten the Indian cook's promise of a horse.

Only problem was, I'd gotten used to talking to Sister Harford and hearing about Getty Coleman through her. I didn't reflect on it then, but I was coming to love the two of them, and when I thought of leaving, it hurt, and so I kept putting it off.

One day she waited around the homestead until I came out to talk to her. That was unusual. She generally left it up to me as to whether we'd speak or not. But I came out, and she said, "Getty Coleman means to speak with you again if you'll let him."

"Sure," I said.

"He said he'd like to see you tomorrow if possible."

"Is it safe?" I asked her.

"We—I mean—I believe so. Brother Coleman thought that Gibson's men were watching him ever since he purchased that coat for you. But lately things have quieted down. He's very concerned about your situation. I've told him all that I've seen of you, but he would like to see you himself again."

"Oh," I said. "Do you see Brother Coleman that much?"

She colored pink all the way from her chin to her hair. Her mouth got straighter than usual, but her eyes were all flustered. "At the church services, of course," she said. "Nothing else."

"Oh, I see."

"And of course my brother has stock in Coleman's cattle, but that's all," she added. "Nothing more."

"Where should I meet him?" I asked her.

The question pulled her out of some other train of thought. She actually stammered. "Uh—where you met before. Does—does that make sense?"

"Yup. Where he gave me the venison?" I asked.

"Yes, that's the place. The venison. Tomorrow."

She got into her two-seater all flustered. I didn't know what I'd said.

By this time it had been six or seven weeks since Coleman and I had met the first time, and I trusted him. But that was my undoing. I trusted Coleman but had forgotten about all my other enemies.

Those men of Gibson's had pulled back from watching Coleman, knowing that once they did, he'd come right to me. It was the kind of trick that Pa'd never have fallen for, but I did.

Spring was coming and the ice was melting. That was what saved my life, I reckon. The water was rising in the cave, not too quickly and not too high yet, but

I spent a good piece of time moving my things to higher ground in the cave, farther from the stream.

I spent a lot longer on the chores than I meant to, losing track of time in the cave like I always did. That was the exact thing that saved me, because if I'd been thinking, I would have left early, and when I got ambushed, it would have been before Coleman arrived.

As it was, Coleman was already waiting for me down lower, under cover, on the lookout on my behalf. I came scurrying out of the stand of trees that hid my secret entrance and started slogging my way through slush and water down toward the place where we'd met. I was almost there when one of Gibson's boys who was sitting perched above to watch for me let me have it in the back with a revolver.

The slug tore into my left shoulder blade, but it felt like it had gone into my heart. I yelled out when it hit me and heard the man above me yell, "I got him!"

Then there was answering fire ahead of me as I pitched forward face down into the slush, and I thought I'd seen the last of life on this side of eternity.

But when I next opened my eyes, Coleman was dragging me to cover.

"Go on," I said. "It's too bad."

He'd driven off the one who'd shot me. But there'd be more coming.

Coleman probed with his fingers along my back. I was faint from the shot, but I gasped, "Coleman, don't get shot for me. Get out of here."

"You're going to get us both shot if you don't keep quiet," he said. I fainted dead away after that. When I woke up, he was holding me upright in his arms off the slushy ground, with both of us propped behind a tree for cover. I couldn't talk because the pain was too bad and I was bleeding hard.

"We're going to run for it," he said in my ear. "His partners haven't got up to him yet." But the words seemed to just slide right over me without ever going in. I didn't know what was happening.

After that I saw a confused jumble of the ground and horse's hooves and Sister Harford's face, and then the beams of a ceiling. And it seemed that I felt the roughness of a cloth on my face. It chapped my lips up bad.

Finally my senses came back to me, and I opened my eyes. I was in a little room with quilts hung all over the furniture, and there were warming pans and bricks in the bed with me. It was right crowded in there.

Sister Harford was in the room, spreading one of the quilts over me. She didn't notice that I was awake until I spoke up.

"Where am I?" I asked her. I sounded weak and tired, even to myself.

"In hiding," she said, as though she took care of shot people all the time. "You're in the upstairs of my house, and Gibson's men think that you're at Coleman's place."

"My lips are chapped up."

She brought a little tin of beeswax and immediately applied some to my lips. Right handy, she was.

"Brother Coleman and I had to stifle your cries. The wound became infected before we could get the bullet out, and he had to cut it open again."

The thought sent the shakes through me, but I couldn't remember any of it. "Will it be all right?" I whispered.

"We've seared it and dressed it." She nodded. "It will be all right."

I wanted to ask her a lot more, but the ceiling was looking swirly again, so I hushed up until it settled down.

"It's chilly up here, but I dare not keep you downstairs," she told me. I realized that she was running quilts and bed warmers up and downstairs for me—that was why all the quilts were everywhere. "We fear that once Gibson's men realize that you're not at Coleman's, they might look here. We want this place to seem as normal as possible. You must be very quiet, if you can."

"Yes ma'am." She and Coleman were doing a lot for me. Even after I'd told her what I really thought about the Lord.

She bustled out again. I passed into sleep.

Chapter 17

The River Breaks Up

Sister Harford prayed regularly with me and read the Bible to me every day. At first I was so grateful to be in a real house that all I could do was look at the place and at her and feel glad. But of course the situation was still pretty grim, and I got to thinking about that and wondering what I could do to save my skin.

She was a pretty brisk one, always whisking in and out and keeping the room tidy and me as warm as possible. She didn't let me get the mopes, which I certainly would have done.

By saying that she didn't let me get the mopes, I don't mean that she sat by my bed holding my hand and telling me that everything would be all right. Instead of that, if she saw I was drooping, she'd tell me that I should be ashamed of myself. Sometimes I got needled with her, but she insisted I hadn't a thing in the world to be gloomy over. I was at last in a decent house and I was alive.

I did get right vexed with her at one point and told her to her face that she was an ornery cuss and no wonder she was still a spinster. She came right back and said that the minute I could get to my feet she was going to learn me some manners. With a hickory switch.

Well, I was ashamed of myself as soon as the words popped out of my mouth. It'd seemed natural with Pa to go back and forth with him. But with Sister Harford, I knew I'd spoken out of turn as soon as I said it. I'd never realized before how mean I could talk.

After that she got right vexed with me herself and marched on down the stairs and wouldn't come back up again either. I was warm enough, and the room was tidy, so I didn't need her that way.

I got to feeling worse and worse over what I'd said, and I wanted to apologize. But she wouldn't come up. I waited for what seemed forever, and the room got cold and dim, and then I got scared. I called to her, but she didn't answer.

I thought sure she was doing something and hadn't heard me. So I waited a few minutes and called her, but when she didn't come again I got scared—not of anything happening, but that she was leaving me alone, and I couldn't stand the thought of being so alone again. So I really called her, and I begged her, and in the end, I threw myself right out of the bed. It was almost a regular fit, and at the first sound of it she had hurried to come up, except I'd worked myself into such a state that I didn't hear her on the step.

I believe I said earlier that all my emotions since Pa died were like a river in ice, but that ice had been breaking up, and this was the moment the river overflowed. I didn't know where she was, or why it had gotten so dark. I was a renegade in a cave, with my shoulder on fire from having fallen on it so hard.

At last when I came to myself again from the fit, she was alongside me and was rocking me, favoring the bad shoulder.

"Don't leave me again, don't leave me again. I'll be good," I told her.

"Josiah," she said. I had turned her all weepy, but when she settled down, she said, "I didn't mean to frighten you like that."

"It got dark, that's all," I said.

"I didn't realize that the dark frightened you."

"It doesn't. I live in the dark. I live in a cave."

She took me by the chin, half-tender and half-brisk. "Not anymore."

"Yes I do. I live in a cave."

"Come up to the bed. I'll bring lamps for you." She helped me into the bed again, pulled the covers around me, and bustled out to get light.

"I live in a cave," I said after her retreating figure. "Where are you going?"

"I'll bring you a lamp or two; I'll be right there," she said. "Listen and you'll hear me coming up the steps."

I did as she said and heard her that time. It was almost all right again. I was back in her house. But what had I said in my fit? I'd said all kinds of things about Pa, and the money, and the horses dying, and the homestead.

She set a lamp down on the table by my bed. "There. Isn't that nice?" She bent down and kissed my forehead. Those prim lips of hers trembled a mite. That was my first notion that she might not be so brisk as she let on.

"What'd I say to you?" I asked. "I'm sorry."

"Josiah, I forgive you. It's all right. I'm sorry I was so long coming."

"Did they hang my Pa, or was he burned?"

She may have thought I was raving again, because she looked real soberly into my eyes a minute. Then she said, "He was hung, Josiah."

"Where'd they bury him?" I asked.

"They brought the body to town, and the minister took it up to the Hill and buried it."

"They're going to lynch me too."

"They'll have to lynch me first, Josiah," she promised. "I won't let them hurt you. If they force the matter, we'll take it to court and prove that you're innocent."

"Gibson wants the money," I told her. "Pa's life's savings. But—but there ain't no such thing. It was just a rumor. There's no money, Sister."

"Your Pa's savings belong to you," she said.

"There ain't any," I said again. "I don't want any money, and there ain't none anyway."

"Then you're safe."

"No, Gibson thinks I've got it. He won't let it go to court. He and his hands have already tried me. They'll get past the sheriff."

"The Lord is my helper. I will not fear what man may do," she recited.

"Will you stay here a while?" I asked.

"Yes. I'm right here. Go to sleep, my boy." She smoothed my hair back on my forehead. Even though I wasn't raving anymore and was minded to fall asleep, I felt tears trickling out of my eyes.

"Pa never did care nothing about me," I said with my eyes shut. "And now he's dead. It's too late."

"God makes all things new, Josiah," she whispered. But when I opened my eyes, I saw that she was crying herself, real soft so that I wouldn't have known unless I opened my eyes and looked. "God makes all things new."

Chapter 18

Getty Coleman Again

Sister Harford had to know that I didn't really have religion. That was dreadfully uncomfortable, because I'd passed myself off at the Home as having religion. I never had meant to lie about anything. I'd worked pretty hard at religion, I thought, but I wondered what she was thinking of me.

The next day she got right back to being brisk, except she kept the lamp by my bed all the time. And she wasn't quite so stern. She generally sat by me a while every night until I fell asleep.

One stormy day Getty Coleman managed to sneak away and come visit. I was as glad to see him as if he'd been a king.

By then my shoulder was better, and I was pretty well recovered from the fever that had come with getting shot. I was able to hobble around the upstairs by day, and at night when the curtains were drawn, I'd come downstairs.

"Soon as you're able, you'll come out and live with me on my spread," he promised me. "Then if there's talk of a lynching, why, we'll see just what Gibson means to do."

Coleman's ranch was pretty good sized, and I knew he was counting on his men fighting off Gibson's if it came to a ranch war.

Ranch wars weren't all that common. Cowboys generally preferred kicking up their heels together over shooting each other. But Bart Gibson had a purpose in this war.

"Gibson thinks I've got a big parcel of money from Pa," I said.

"Yup. Th' word is you're sitting on twenty thousand dollars," he told me. "But there's always been talk that your Pa had a big pile of money hid some place."

I shook my head. "Ain't no money, Mr. Coleman. That's just a rumor. Pa was broke except for that homestead. But Gibson'll never believe that."

Sister Harford shot a quick glance at Coleman when I told him that. I wondered if she thought I was lying. I was lying, but maybe not for the reason you're thinking. I didn't want the money. I just felt sure that if I let Gibson get it, there'd be blood shed over it. There had been all the way up to this point. Other folks would fight him for it, and then they'd fight each other. And besides, it might make me look like I really had been Pa's accomplice in whatever folks said he'd done. I intended to believe and act like there was no money.

"Well, money or no money, we'll have to sit tight a while longer," he said. "Then when you're more able, I'll bring you out to my place. We'll make room for you out there."

"You been mighty nice to me," I said. "I don't mean to make your ranch a battlefield."

"You won't," he said. "If Gibson pushes to get hold of you, he'll be bringing down any gunfire on himself."

He glanced a little more sharply at me. "You know that when Gibson gets his wheels moving, the sheriff ain't got no power."

That was the sad truth about lots of western towns. Vigilante justice had made the West safe in lots of ways. There'd been few lawmen, and some of the first ones were mighty corrupt. But the big ranchers and rich men could turn vigilante justice to suit themselves. And sometimes a town might end up with two or three different groups of vigilantes, each group accusing the other of being corrupt. Then they'd all shoot it out or fight it out until the town was half-razed. Whoever came out standing declared his group the only honest one, and things went on from there.

If Gibson got his most powerful hired men agreed on a plan, they could easily get his other hands stirred up, and those hands could likely stir up half the town. That's how they'd come to hang Pa. Coleman's best defense was to bring me to his place, where we could at least fight a pitched battle. That would cool the courage of most of the town folks, at least.

I still wasn't happy about bringing all this trouble on Getty Coleman. It put me into a blue mood to think on it, but just then Coleman said to Sister Harford, "Well, with the revival beginning next week, the town may have other things on its mind. Maybe after the first week or so, we might find our chance to get him out to my spread."

"Revival coming to town?" I asked.

They both nodded.

"Ought to last at least a month," Coleman guessed. "Generally the town settles down for at least a while after a revival."

"Are you both going to the meetings?" I asked.

I didn't mean both going together to the meetings, and Coleman didn't take it that way. He just said, "Yes. There'd be a lot of suspicion from Gibson's men if I didn't show. And if Sister Harford didn't show, they might just figure out she has company."

But Sister Harford colored right up again and was mighty embarrassed. That prim mouth of hers just got straighter and straighter until there was almost nothing but white space between nose and chin.

I started to put things together. I suppose a spinster and a bachelor who were so regular at church had attracted the notice of a lot of folks. Maybe there was a notion going around that the two of them should get hitched.

Anyway, she stumbled out with a word or two about getting us tea, and Coleman looked after her and shook his head.

"Right smart woman," he said under his breath, using *smart* like some folks use *pretty*. "For her age, don't you think?"

"Sure," I said.

He let out a heavy breath and went back to talking about the move to his ranch. But the truth hit me. I'd been wondering if she was sweet on Coleman. But that was backwards. It was Coleman who was sweet on her. She was just embarrassed by it.

I thought about it for only a second or two. While Coleman talked, I laid my own plans in my head.

I sure didn't mean to start a ranch war. And I didn't mean to get lynched.

But that revival had given me an idea. When a revival comes to town, folks are always on the lookout for wayward lambs to welcome into the fold. And decent folks don't hang wayward lambs who come into the fold. Josiah Eagle was going back into religion. In a big way.

Chapter 19

More on Sister Harford

I enjoyed coming downstairs at night. Sister Harford would draw the curtains and pull in the latchstring on the back door, and it was safe, so long as I was quiet.

Her brother had a place about ten miles out from town. He was prosperous and had a wife and a passel of kids. In the evenings she would tell me all about growing up back East. Their family had money, and Sister Harford had invested most of hers in his cattle. She'd come out—it seemed, from what she said—to have somebody to be near to. I reckon maybe she'd been thinking some on marriage.

But Sister Harford wasn't what you'd call meek and dependent. I guess nobody that she'd met had shaped up to what she'd had in mind. And she got interested in "civilizing" the town. A big piece of her money had gone into the church building, and by and by I came to see that she was behind just about every charity that ran through the church. She'd had a hand in the Boys Home too. She and Sister Erlis and the others were mighty thick, and they visited when the weather was good.

She also had a shelf of books in her parlor, and she let me read them. I read *Ivanhoe* right off, and I got so interested in it that I almost got fever again from staying up late to see what happened. She didn't scold me, but she said I could read only thirty pages a day. I felt that was right ornery of her, but I didn't say so. I just kept it to thirty pages a day.

Meanwhile, she made me new clothes to wear—even a broadcloth suit. When I tried it on, she called me handsome, and I smiled at her. I felt handsome, but if I'd said it, I'd have gotten the pride preached out of me, so I kept my mouth shut.

My shoulder and back were still some sore from that bullet, but I could move around as long as I favored the arm. I couldn't lift or tote much, but I did what I could to help her with the housework. And I didn't complain, neither. We'd all pitched in with chores at the Home, and I was used to it.

It was while I was setting at her kitchen table, reading and waiting to jump up and lend her a hand if she asked, that she suddenly said, "My, it will be so quiet when you leave, Josiah. I wonder what I shall do."

"It won't be quiet long once Gibson gets wind of me," I said.

"Are you feeling sorry for yourself?" she asked briskly.

"I'm saying that I'd rather get shot away from here, but I'd rather not get shot at all. Or lynched," I added. "I'd stay right here with you if I could."

She came right over to me and dropped her hands on my good shoulder. "Would you really?"

I looked up at her. "Sure. Ain't you ever loved anybody?"

She looked like she didn't know whether to laugh or to cry. "Of course I have. Haven't I told you endless stories about my family? I love them dearly." For once the straight line of her mouth set easy, and her eyes got moist. She still missed them, after all these years.

I felt embarrassed. It was nothing new for her to love people. It was only new to me. "I never did," I said, kind of stammering. "I do now, and I don't want to leave." I looked down.

"But you love Brother Coleman. Every time you talk about him or see him, your whole face brightens up. And he loves you."

I nodded. "What I hate," I admitted, "is thinking of Gibson hurting you or shooting Coleman. That night I was yelling for you, I should have remembered how dangerous it was to make that much noise."

"No harm came of it. And part of being friends and Christian brothers and sisters means running risks for each other and with each other, Josiah," she told me. "If you admire knights like Ivanhoe, then you must grant Getty Coleman the right to do the same thing—to defend you when you're innocent."

"If he or you was to be hurt in this—it would be worse than Pa," I told her, and my voice broke. "Because you've helped me."

"God is our refuge and our strength," she said gently. "He'll protect us, Josiah. The name of the Lord is a strong tower. The righteous runneth into it and is safe."

"Will Gibson go to the revival?" I asked.

"He probably will. At least the first week. He would consider it respectable."

"Most of the people go the first week?"

"Most of the people who think of themselves as being respectable—yes," she said. "It's a break from the normal routine."

I pondered on what would be the best night to make my move.

"You won't be—be nervous when I'm gone in the evenings?" she asked. She was still worried that I was afraid of being alone.

"No, I'll be all right."

"Josiah, do you still think about the Lord the same way that you thought about Him when you were living in that cave?"

I looked up at her. She didn't look prim, only real tender and kind.

"I been thinking about the Lord lately," I told her.

"You're not saying that to make me happy, are you?"

"No, I have been thinking on Him." That much was true enough, I reckon.

"What have you been thinking?" she asked.

"How nice it would be to be one of God's children," I said. In a sense, that was true too, except I'd decided I'd never get a chance to be one. But I didn't tell her that.

"It is nice," she said. "He takes care of His children, Josiah. Do you understand that Jesus died for all of your sins?"

"Will God protect me if I go to the revival meetings?" I asked her that to get her off the subject.

The question set her back. At last she said, "We'll have to ask the Lord to show us the answer to that."

I nodded, and she didn't say anything more.

Chapter 20

Revival

By Sister Harford's and Brother Coleman's accounts, the revival meetings were getting right enthusiastic. The preacher that came was young and had lots of energy, and he started right in on Sabbath-breaking and drinking whiskey. He preached fire against sin, and he told about salvation free to all.

This was the kind of preacher that came only once in a lifetime, I reckon—the sort that my Pa would have come after with a shotgun. And from the accounts around town, some of the men were talking about riding him out on a rail. But he kept right on going, and by Thursday night, some of the old drunks from the saloon went forward and got religion.

That changed the whole state of things. Other folks started perking up. By Saturday night the church was crowded with some folks looking for religion and others looking to see who else was going to walk the aisle. I was still biding my time. The town was about ready for a miraculous conversion, and I meant to give them one. I didn't half-expect the Lord to care if a renegade like me got religion, but I knew it would swing folks' opinions into my favor. Sunday came and was quieter, though the church was still crowded.

Monday night Sister Harford went out, and pretty soon the street got quiet and dark. While she was at the meeting, I had to keep the lamps out and be still. But that night after she left, I climbed out the back window and went after her to the church, which was set at the edge of town.

The night was dark, and the church windows had lamps in them, with swirls of smoke curling against the glass panes. There was quite a crowd inside. Things were still jacking up, as far as attendance and interest from the town folks were concerned, instead of winding down. I had a lot of respect for that preacher for not getting chased out by the rougher folk.

Well, I wasn't wearing my broadcloth, but I wasn't in rags, either, so for a minute nobody paid me any mind as I pushed my way inside. The congregation was singing "Must Jesus Bear the Cross Alone," and Sister Harford was up about the middle of the church, hemmed in with people.

I was glad of that, because I wasn't going to own publicly that she'd been the one to take me in. It would have brought her trouble.

But then after a few seconds a kind of intake of breath went all around me, and I heard whispering, and people started poking each other and whispering more. Gibson was sitting closer to the back than Sister Harford, and he turned around when someone tapped him. He had his wife and daughters with him, so I knew he wouldn't get too feisty. But he looked at me sharp, and I looked back at him as blank as I could.

Getty Coleman was way up near the front, and when he turned around, he looked startled at the sight of me. I think he would have come back to me, but he had too much respect for the service to interrupt it so.

"Now," the preacher said as the hymn ended, "all who know the blessed virtue of the cross, sing with me: 'On a hill far away, stood an old rugged cross, the emblem of suffering and shame. . . .'"

Some of them folks joined in right hearty, but since he didn't give a number or set the tune, others could only stand there.

He was a fairly young preacher, but he sang like he had a throat full of gravel. He'd preach hard and then bust into a hymn, and then he'd preach some more. I was only half-listening, though I made myself look mighty intent. Not that I wasted another thought on Gibson—I didn't. But the whole scene captured my interest. Of course I'd been to worship at the Home, but this was different. I'd never been to a revival before.

And at the Home the preacher would tailor down all his sermons for the young ones, so I'd heard mostly about Moses and Joshua and David. Every now and then somebody would get around to grace, but not as often as you'd think, and I'd never paid much attention out there.

The first thing that struck me about this preacher was that he backed up every thought with a verse of Scripture. I wondered how anybody could know a book as big as the Bible that well. I got lost in wondering about that while he preached, and I took to counting every time he used a new verse.

Then the next hymn started, and I took a pause to look around again. Most everybody knew I was there, and I saw Sister Harford looking over at me, worried. I tried to stay blank for her too, because I didn't want folks to know that we were acquainted. I did start to worry a mite—that I'd bit off more than I could chew in showing up—and I almost missed my cue. The invitation started.

"Come brother, come," the preacher was saying. "Jesus will make room. Oh brother, sister, come to the bench and pray."

I'd been meaning to go right down, but I decided to wait a bit. Right away some other folks went forward, and it was just my luck that one of them was weeping as he went. That got the crowd going. They were ready for a big conversion.

It cuts me like a knife now to write this story out and tell the callous way I played them all, even the sincere ones. I'm not such a fool that I don't know that plenty of folks did what I did that night—faked a conversion for their own sake. But it chills me now. Such folks play with fire and often as not get themselves convinced that they really did something, when all they did was repeat a prayer.

But I waited until the crowd was fairly surging and half of them had tears on their faces, and then I stumbled up the aisle and fell on my knees at the mourners' bench. That produced quite a stir, and not half a minute later one of the church elders fell on his knees beside me.

"What is it, boy?" he asked.

"Oh deacon, help me," I sobbed. "Help me, 'cause I don't know how to pray!"

He put his arm around me. "Jesus ain't looking for high and mighty words, son. He's lookin' for a contrite heart. Do you know what *contrite* means? It means to be sorry."

"Deacon, I done some awful things—" I gasped. "I'm Josiah Eagle's boy, Josiah Eagle!"

"I know that." He went on and on, and I cried and clung to him until the folks in the front pews were right moved at sight of me.

"Pray for this lost one," the preacher said to them. "Pray for the Lord to give him light!"

Even Getty Coleman was down on his knees, and I think in a way that the Lord answered that preacher's prayer, while I was right in the midst of playing with blasphemy. Because right then I saw clear as a bell that it was God who had brought Coleman to my rescue—He really had been merciful to me. It was like a flash of pain in my heart to think of what I was doing to Coleman, to play-act this way, and my conscience said to me, "You were always honest about being a renegade, at least, but now you're lying. You're lying to your only two friends." I wasn't worth them. I wasn't worth the man kneeling by me.

"It's to save them," I told myself, but the pang lasted, and I got a sweat on me while the deacon by my side prayed. I was sure that even though God had started to have mercy on me, He was really mad at me now.

But I went through with it and got religion again. I prayed alongside the deacon and threw in about every catch phrase I'd heard him utter. I prayed until I knew he was ready to back me up to the end that I had religion same as any other man in that congregation.

"I'll reform," I promised God. But that pang wouldn't quite go away.

Chapter 21

Deacon Staves

"Who is this lost lamb?" the preacher asked as the deacon brought me up before him. Some folks were already filing out of the crowded church, but others were still there, watching us.

"Josiah Eagle," the deacon said. "The son of a renegade that was lynched last summer."

"Oh, my boy," the preacher exclaimed, and right there he embraced me. "A life of toil and sorrow. You've eaten the bread of bitterness, haven't you?"

"Yes sir," I gulped, and I really was moved. No reproach from him, and no scorn.

"Jesus makes all things new, my boy. Rest on Him now." But he clung to me real tight, and I realized that somehow he genuinely understood some of what I must have been through.

"Preacher," I began, and I think there was something in my heart that would have spoken the truth to him, but it died again.

"Yes, Josiah?" he asked, and looked at me.

"I got no family," I told him. "And I don't want to be a renegade."

He frowned in thought a minute and would have spoken, but then the deacon interrupted.

"Preacher," he said, "don't you fret. We got room for this boy. He can help keep the store for us, and we'll set him on the straight and narrow path. I promise before God, me and my wife will look after him."

Well, lots of people heard that, and they took to weeping again, and even I was struck by the offer. Mighty kind, all right. For a second I thought I really had got religion at last, and my luck was turning in my favor.

"God bless you, Brother Staves," the preacher said. "Do you give your word before the Lord that you'll do right by this boy and raise him in the fear and admonition of the Lord?"

"I sure do, preacher. Nance, you come up here and stand with me," he said to his wife.

She was just as weepy as the rest, and she came up too, and they both promised to care for me.

I shot one glance over at Sister Harford, but she kept herself mum. She did look a bit weepy herself, and her mouth was set so straight and tight I didn't know if she was happy and trying to hide it, or sad and trying to hide it.

When I looked at the back of the church, I saw that Gibson was gone.

It took a right long time for the church to empty out and for folks to quit staring at me, but pretty soon the Staves and me and Sister Harford met together.

"I have been looking after Josiah," she told them.

"You've always been kind to wayward sheep," Deacon Staves told her. "But you've reaped from your sowing tonight, Sister."

"Yes," she nodded and looked at me.

"Thank you," I said to her. "Is this all right with you?"

She nodded. "You should have a good home with a good father, Josiah. And you'll be nearby. Getty asked me to look after you because he had to get back to the ranch. But I think this is for the best. School will be nearby too."

I kind of thought that night that Sister Harford had her doubts about what I did, but I was determined to set her mind at ease.

Once I got my few things moved over to Deacon Staves's store, I began life in earnest as a Christian.

They lived up above the store, and there was a spare room for me. Deacon Staves started me in school, and like I said, I worked my best to please him and his wife. And to set my conscience at rest.

Mornings I took down the shutters in the store and rekindled the fire in the store's stove before setting out for school. There were only about twenty pupils in the school, and I stayed mostly to myself. But I was quiet and obedient and always knew my lessons for the teacher. When I got home from school, I'd help in the store. There might be unpacking to do, or ciphering up of accounts, or things to deliver. Nights after supper I'd stay at my books at the kitchen table.

Deacon Staves was as good as pie. From the first he showed me how to handle money and everything and never mistrusted me at all. And he talked long with me about things. I told him all about Pa and what I'd seen in life and what I'd done. He never did ask about the money, but I told him two things: one, I'd never had a hand in robbing folks, and two, there wasn't any money. The first was true, and the second I wanted to be true.

He believed me on both counts.

The story of my conversion was a regular nine days' wonder. I do believe folks would come into the store in the afternoons just to see me and talk to me. And meanwhile, Sister Erlis sent word to confirm that I'd been at the Home during those supposed robberies. She'd been saying it ever since Pa got killed, but at last folks started listening to her.

Taking it all in all, it looked like things were settling down at last. I even started to be happy.

Deacon and Missus got fond of me, and we had some pleasant evenings together there at the winter's end. I did start to learn the Bible in earnest too. In that sense I wasn't very happy because I would read it and start to realize that I still wasn't a part of Christian people—not really. But then I'd tell myself that I sort of was too. I'd prayed—I'd even cried. And just about everybody thought I was saved.

I visited Sister Harford on Saturdays and did some wood chopping for her, as well as some other heavy chores. She always had cookies for me and was right pleased to see me.

Getty Coleman would ride into town about once every two weeks and visit me at the store. He was as good as a man could be, I believe, and he loved me like a son. I was mindful of all he'd done for me, and I was even more grateful to him than to Sister Harford. That was when it got hardest to keep my secret doubts secret. Something always told me that if I just up and told Coleman the whole truth—both about the money and about thinking I didn't really have religion after all—that he'd help me. But then I wondered if there was any hope for my soul. What if Coleman told me there wasn't? And what if a whole new war started over the money?

For a while the surface of things did stay smooth, but then word came around that the sheriff was looking to do things lawfully, and that I ought to go to trial.

Well, I knew who was stirring up that trouble: Gibson.

"If he's so set on the law, why don't we get the law to look into who it was that murdered my Pa!" I exclaimed one day to Deacon Staves. It was right after one of the Gibson hands had come in and told me all this to my face.

Deacon grabbed me real quick—so quick I thought he was going to hit me. That was the way Pa acted before I got a beating.

"Don't you never say that, Josiah!" he exclaimed.

I looked him in the eye—and my own eyes were real big from being startled. But I shook my head. "It's true, Deacon. Lynching's murder just the same as back-shooting a man. They murdered him."

"Josiah, what are you telling me?" he asked. He was a big and bony man, all weather-beaten in the face, with a droopy gray mustache. "Boy, do you think I don't know it was murder?" he asked me. "It was murder, and it was murder they meant to do to you too. Don't say another word like that, boy."

He let me go.

"Why not?" I asked him. "You know it's true, then."

He looked back at me, and then he went up and closed and locked the front door and pulled down the curtain. We were alone in the empty store.

"You always lived out of town," he told me. "You holed yourself up in that there Home." He shook his head. "Oh, Josiah, when this here town got stirred up to go hang your Pa, most decent folks locked themselves in their houses. But the others went—why? Because Bart Gibson told them to. Some wanted a share in the money, and some went because they got stirred up, and others went just because Gibson said it was time to go. He's powerful, boy. A sight more powerful than you or me or anybody else."

"You're afraid of him," I said.

"We're all afraid of him. Even the sheriff."

I shook my head. "What about God?" I asked. "Isn't He supposed to help you folks?" Deacon didn't notice my slip there. He just shook his head.

"The Lord forgive me for cowardice, Josiah. But don't speak out agin Gibson. He'll bring it back down onto all our heads."

Chapter 22

Trouble Again

It was me that actually brought the trouble to a head. The spring came on full warm, and town got livelier. The school teacher came down sick with some kind of passing consumption, and we had a week off from school.

I took to doing a real thorough cleaning of the store for Deacon Staves. I was down there all through the day, and so one afternoon when Getty Coleman walked in, he broke into a real big smile.

"Josiah!" he exclaimed. "You playing hookey?"

"School's closed a few days," I told him. "Wait right here. I been cleaning and found some traps I want you to see. You might could use them."

I went into the back room to get the traps, and no sooner did I walk out when Bart Gibson came through the front door and spotted Coleman.

Gibson was wearing a gun, which wasn't unusual, but Coleman was unarmed.

"Coleman, I was hoping I wouldn't have to see you again," Gibson said.

"What brings you here?" Coleman asked him. Gibson generally sent his foreman to get supplies.

"I've come to give that young snake one last chance," Gibson said. "If he'll 'fess up and clear out, there won't be no bloodshed."

"I reckon by 'fess up, you mean tell you where his pa hid all that money 'fore you killed him."

I came to the door of the back room at this and saw Gibson clear his coat off his hip. "Coleman, don't you talk to me that way. Whether you're armed or not," Gibson said.

"If you're plannin' on murderin' Josiah, you're gonna have to gun me down sooner or later," Coleman told him. "Might as well be now."

Deacon kept a rifle in the back of the store in case of robberies. I pulled it off the wall and stepped out. "Gibson," I said.

He looked at me, and his hand twitched.

"Don't you try it," I said. "Keep them hands high."

He picked up his hands.

"Mighty lucky for you I got religion," I told him. "'Cause there's a lot of me that wants to pull this trigger."

"Josiah," Getty Coleman said. "Don't, boy! Don't say them things."

"Drop the gun belt, Gibson," I told him. "And do it slow."

Gibson did as I said, and the whole time his face was like chalk, and he didn't make a sound. I reckon he was brave enough in a pitched battle, but looking up the barrel of a rifle has unnerved many a man. And he knew all that he'd put me through.

"Don't you never threaten Getty Coleman again," I told him. "And don't you never set foot in this store again. Religion or not, if I ever see you step across that threshold, I'll shoot you. You hear me?"

He just looked at me, and I yelled, "Did you hear me?"

"Yes," he said.

"Then back out real slow. I'll be here with this gun all day, so don't try to force your way back in. Now get out."

He backed out, and after a second or two we heard his booted feet clumping away up the dirt main street.

Getty Coleman let out his breath. "You spoke fierce, Josiah," he said.

"I'll not stand by while any man threatens to pull a gun on you, Brother Coleman. Gibson ain't fit to shine your shoes."

I was still wary, standing in the doorway of the backroom and watching the street through the front window.

Coleman shook his head. "Gibson won't come on the sly to get you, Josiah. He'll bring in all his men and make a show of it. But you can believe—after this—that he's gonna try to get you. He'll never forgive you for putting his face in the dirt."

I looked at Getty Coleman. "Are you afraid of him too?" I asked. "You? Of all people? That nearly got kilt for me when I was shot?"

"I'm afraid for you, Son. Not for me," Coleman said. "He won't rest till he has you. He thinks you know where that money is."

"There ain't no money," I said. "All that was just talk."

He shook his head. "No, I believe there was money. Gibson wouldn't follow so hard after something he ain't sure of. He saw it or heard of it somehow. When your Pa took to drinking hard, he'd say anything to anybody.

He may have bragged something he shouldn't have bragged. He may have showed somebody something that he shouldn't ever have showed."

I didn't make answer to that. All I said was "Well, spent or not spent, Pa made a lot of money in his life. He done all of it illegal too. Any money of his is blood money, I reckon, and best forgotten."

"Gibson won't forget." He looked awful sober and worried. "I've half a mind to take you out to the ranch with me."

"No, Brother Coleman. He'd burn out half the town lookin' for me, and I'm responsible for Sister Harford."

His face looked pained on that. "Josiah, I could look out for her too. But she won't say yes."

So what I'd figured was true. He'd been courting her. Or trying to.

"Folks our age ought not behave like children, she told me," he said. "Our age is no age to be setting up house." He sighed and shot a second look at me. "But I saw her with you. She never figured how pleasant it might be to set up house. Or how she might like taking care of someone."

"Well, why don't you ask her again, now she knows better?" I asked him.

"Because she made me promise never to say another word about it to her, boy! And what if I should risk it and offend her?"

I shook my head. "Brother Coleman, I think any woman who'd turn you down is foolish, but maybe you ought to try a younger one." Out west, lots of gray-haired men would marry younger women. It took a man lots of years to build up a home good enough for a good woman.

But it was his turn to shake his head. "I don't love a younger woman, Josiah. I love her. And when Gibson was standing there ready to draw on me, it struck me that maybe that was what it'd take to bring her around. I sure love her."

"It's no good if she gets her head on straight after you been shot," I said. "But maybe she'll come 'round yet."

It was just then that Deacon Staves came in from the depot. One look at me, Coleman, and the gun belt on the floor told him a lot. He went pale. "What's happened?" he asked.

Brother Coleman told him the story.

"Josiah, Josiah!" he exclaimed. "You're bringing ruin and trouble onto yourself and us all!"

The words weren't harsh, only frightened, but they brought a rush of red to my cheeks.

"Josiah saved my life," Coleman said softly.

"For the moment, Getty, for the moment," he added. "What's to become of us if this goes on? Gibson won't be denied."

"Deacon Staves, I'm a Christian man," Getty Coleman told him. "But I'd give my vote to fight him—guns against guns. He's bent on overthrowing the sheriff—which he himself put up—and putting up a new one handier to his whims. We got to fight him now, or this town's always gonna be under his thumb."

"Fight?" Deacon asked. "Getty, I fought. You know I fought. But those days are over. I got a wife. I got a home."

"But you won't if Gibson ever gets the notion that your wife or your home is standing in his way," Coleman told him.

Deacon paused a whole long moment, and for the first time I realized that I was seeing a man in his weakness wrestle with something outside himself. Not just his conscience. There was something better and braver than Deacon Staves holding him to the truth in Coleman's words.

"You're right," he said at last. "I'm sorry, Josiah. I didn't mean to shame you. We got to fight him, come what may."

"I ain't gonna stay and put you and Missus in danger," I told him.

"Please, stay," he asked me. "I gave my word to God to care for you, boy, and I love you almost like a son now."

But I shook my head again. "Deacon, there is one person in this here town that ain't one lick scared of Gibson. That's where I'll go for the time being."

"Who is that?" Deacon asked me.

Coleman glanced at me and back at the Deacon. "Sister Harford," he said.

I nodded.

Chapter 23

The Old Indian

My stay at Sister Harford's didn't last long. I hadn't figured it would, and I'd been leery of dragging her into this trouble. But on the other hand, she had a sight more nerve than just about anybody in that town except for Getty Coleman. If trouble came, I didn't want to be standing shoulder to shoulder with somebody who was going to panic.

And for another thing, I was thinking that Gibson just might try to get me through Sister Harford. I didn't mean to leave her alone if trouble was coming. I was fifteen by then—pretty young—but I was handy enough with a gun.

The sheriff and I had a long talk the next afternoon. He was a man put up to the job through Gibson's influence, but something had happened to him since then. He didn't want to be the tool of another man, and he really did believe in upholding the law.

"The main street of the town can be defended," he told me. "If Gibson should come in to take you by force, we can keep him from it, as long as enough volunteers are willing."

"Are they?" I asked him. "Wouldn't it be better if I just rode out alone and tried to get away?"

"You wouldn't get very far. I'm sure his men are watching the roads. And besides, this fight had to come sooner or later. May as well be now," he said. "A town's got to be run by the law, not by men."

He was right. And not only that, there was such a thing as revenge. Even if I rode out, that wouldn't guarantee that Gibson wouldn't take it out on Getty Coleman or on Sister Harford.

"As for volunteers," he added, "I think most folks think you've changed. I reckon on a good number of the men being willing to defend the town."

After that conversation, I was tensed like a spring, waiting for some sign of trouble, but nothing happened for a week. Gibson's hands were riding in and out the same as usual, and I passed a few every now and then. No hard words went by. Getty Coleman had been coming to town every day, wearing a gun on his hip. But as the tenseness in the town eased off, he got back to his work on the ranch.

Sister Harford just went on with business as usual. I was handy with tools, so I took to working on a bookcase for her, and that kept me busy every minute that I wasn't in school. Building the bookcase took me only one morning, but I was working on some nice carving for the front of it.

Every now and then she caught me taking a real hard look at her, and she'd get flustered.

"Whatever are you thinking?" she'd ask me. "Do you think I'm growing a wart on my nose?"

"Course not," I'd say, and then I'd act like I hadn't been staring. But you know, she was right handsome, even for her age. Finally one day she said she was going to take a hickory switch to me, so I told her the truth.

"Getty Coleman told me he was trying to court you and he thought you was real purty and sweet," I told her. "I've been trying to decide if you're right for each other."

"Oh—you bold, audacious boy!" she said all in one breath. But she was more embarrassed than mad. I got stung at her coloring up and getting embarrassed more than I got stung by her words.

"Handsome for sure," I said, bending back to the stove where I was putting in kindling. "But he don't know sweet, I reckon."

She just stood there, pink in the face, knowing I was teasing her but not knowing what to say.

At last she sputtered, "Getty Coleman is old enough to be your father, young man, and I am old enough to be your mother—"

I looked up at her and grinned, and of course that made her realize what she was saying about being eligible to him.

She started again. "Josiah Eagle, adults will carry on their business just fine without your assistance! As for not knowing sweet, I find that a fine way for you to talk to the woman who has nursed you back to life—"

I stood up real fast and faced her. "And the man who saved my life too," I told her. "You got to do your own business, Miss Harford, but I think you and Getty Coleman are the best people in the whole West. He'll never find another woman worthy of him—and you'll never find another man like Getty Coleman. That's all I'm saying."

She composed herself and looked at me real prim while I went and got a big chunk of hardwood for the stove.

But she was wavering a little. At last she said, "Josiah, I know that you love Getty Coleman, but I must do as I see fit."

I nodded. "Okay, then. But when Gibson comes into this town shooting and burning, there's goin' to be four people ain't scared of him. Sheriff, who's married, and me, who's young, and you and Getty Coleman. An' I'll be glad to die just knowin' I got two friends like you. I hope he can die feeling the same way."

Her primness got even tighter, but I knew her well enough to see that she was struggling not to cry. She must have cared for Coleman, though maybe not the way he wanted her to care. But if I knew Sister Harford, it hurt her to be the cause of his pain. She was prim and feisty, but she was delicate, too, in her feelings. "The point is well taken," she said at last. I went out to get more wood.

We didn't say any more about it, and I felt pretty sure that Coleman had lost out. I felt bad for him.

The second week started fine and quiet, and the weather was warm and sultry—unusual for the time of year.

"Bad thunderstorm this afternoon," Sister Harford said as she saw me to the door on my way to the schoolhouse.

I went home for dinner at noon and went back for the afternoon session. It was warm in the schoolhouse, and everybody felt kind of sleepy. I got to thinking about the mountains and the cave, and I had turned my head to look out the window. I really didn't know I was staring out and daydreaming, but after a few minutes I saw a figure go by on horseback that startled me awake.

Indians and white men don't really ride the same. I know an Indian on horseback when I see him. They ride with the horse, if you know what I mean, while a white man generally just rides on top of one.

Well, it was an Indian that went by, an Indian in old ragged castoffs, with his black and gray hair streaming out behind him, all ragged cut.

It was the same Indian who had let me take a skillet and coffeepot off the chuck wagon.

In an instant I knew trouble was afoot. I just got up and ran out, forgetting the schoolroom, the teacher, and everything. I went pounding out after that Indian and ki-yi'd to him to get his attention. He turned and then wheeled the horse around.

"Josiah Eagle," he said as he rode up, "my life at the Gibson ranch is over."

"Why?" I asked him.

"They are coming tonight to hang you. I have come to warn you and to die."

I shook my head. "Ride with me to Coleman's place. He'll help us. I'll run and warn Sister Harford."

Chapter 24

Coleman Sets Me Straight

Deacon lent me one of his horses, and we rode by Sister Harford's to give her the word.

"Go to Coleman for help," she said right away.

I nodded. "We are. You'll spread the word around?"

"Of course."

My horse sensed excitement and wanted to be off, but I pulled him in and looked down at her. "Remember that time I said you were ornery?"

"Yes." And she nodded. For once she looked real tender and not prim at all.

"You are real ornery," I told her. "Please don't get yourself shot, Sister."

"Josiah Eagle!"

I leaned all the way down from the saddle and kissed her cheek. "I like folks ornery," I said. I straightened back up. "But don't go out there and put yourself in danger."

"Are men the only ones allowed to defend their friends?" she asked me.

"I'll let 'em hang me if I find I ain't got a home to come back to," I told her. I nodded to the Indian. "Let's go."

We raced out of the town for Coleman's place. The Indian gave a sideways glance at me and grunted something. I think he thought that what I'd said to Sister Harford was real funny. But in his own way, he liked both me and her.

It took us about half an hour to ride out to Coleman's, going like there was fire on the horses' tails. We brought them to a skidding stop and dismounted, but on our way in, the Indian said to me—in English—"Woman with no heart like fish with no life. Good for nothing but to put in the ground. Mother has right to die for son. Wife has right to die for husband."

"All that's true," I told him. "And it don't matter what I think anyway, 'cause she's gonna do what she thinks is best."

At the news of trouble, Coleman rousted out his foreman, Curly Rush.

"You git the men and git 'em armed and out to the town," he told Curly. "Hurry 'long, 'cause dark ain't far off. I'll ride back with the boy. Let the old Indian rest. He can come back with you if he has a mind."

Coleman went out to the stable and got his horse, and as we mounted up, he glanced over at me, real keen of eye.

"You ready for this, Son?" he asked.

I looked ahead at the road beyond us and the line of mountains that were beyond the town itself. A big shadowy cloud hung over it all, heavy with rain.

Curly came running out with a gun belt and a six-shooter. He handed them up to me. "All we can spare," he said. "I thought you might need them, Josiah."

Coleman nodded. "May not be time to arm up when we get to town."

"I thank you, Curly," I told him. He nodded and ran back to the bunkhouse.

"I asked you a question, Josiah," Coleman said to me.

I looked at him as I fastened on the belt.

"Coleman," I said. "I want you to know two things: one, I owe you everything and I'd rather be your friend than to be king of the world."

He nodded. "And the other?"

"The other is that I'm a liar through and through. I lied about the money, and I never did get religion. Not like you got it."

"Josiah," he told me. "I never meant to mock you, Son. But I knew the truth on both counts."

I just looked at him.

"Son, when you was in a fever after you got shot, you told Sister Harford and me all about that money, and where it is, and how scared you were of it being found."

"You knew!" I exclaimed.

"Sure, but if you was that scared, we was content to let it lie until you got better. But then before we could talk to you about it, you got religion—or seemed to. But when you kept right on lying about it—well, we figured maybe you was just putting on for folks."

I licked my lips. I could hardly meet his eye. At last I did. "But I ain't lying when I say you're the best friend I ever had, Mister Coleman."

"Josiah, I ain't lying when I say I love you and am ready to go out and fight side by side with you," he told me. "And God ain't lying when He says any man may come to Him and be saved. You're all confused about that—but there's a path every man is invited to walk. Not an aisle."

Daylight was on the wane. We had to go, but I said, "You think there's a way I could be saved? Seems like I was born different from you and the good people. I'm a renegade."

"I want to tell you something," he said, "and the whole town's gonna have to wait on this story. There was a man born right poor. Never saved no money. Never owned a house. And a lot of sinners were His friends. The religious folks and the preachers in His town called Him an outlaw although He never did nothing wrong. They didn't have much to do with Him until the end, when they took Him outside their city and killed Him out where all the renegades were killed. But I love Him."

"Who was He?" I asked.

"That was Jesus, Josiah. You been confused, boy—confusing law-abiding folks with Christian folks and confusing religion with forgiveness. But Jesus came to save sinners, not the righteous. He said so Himself. So if you think you're a rotten sinner, that puts you first in line to be saved."

I just looked at him, kind of stunned from everything he said. He'd read me like a book.

"Let's go," I said at last. I spurred on the horse, and he followed me out. A rain shower was starting as we went out, and the sky had darkened up. Night wasn't far off anyway.

Chapter 25

Face to Face with Gibson

Darkness came down quickly with the rain. It was a steady downpour as we came into the town.

"Ride for Elizabeth Harford's," Coleman told me. "Get her out of there and over to the church or somewhere safe. Gibson must know she put you up in hiding. I want to make sure she's set by safe."

I nodded and went off around the other side of the town. I could hear men yelling from over on the main street, and I realized that the fireworks had already started. All the shutters were closed in the houses, and the back streets were dark.

I swung off the horse and led him up an alley, ground-tied him, and sneaked over to Sister Harford's house. She didn't come when I knocked on the kitchen door, and I saw that the latchstring was pulled in. The house was dark.

I went around to the front, but there was no answer there. She'd gone off somewhere herself or had been taken.

I drew the six-gun and made sure it was loaded. Then I started up the street under the eaves of the houses, watching for signs of her.

I thought she might have gone to Deacon's to sit with Missus. From over on main street there came the noise of steady shots. Sheriff had put up a barricade and was trying to fight off the attack of the Gibson hands. Even if I didn't get lynched that night, I realized that the sheriff likely would. The Gibson hands would say he was crooked.

He'd put his life in danger for me. It was time to go throw in my hand with him. I crossed the street, forgetful of any danger, and a gunshot rang out.

The bullet creased my left leg and I dropped right there in the middle of the street. My back splashed up a wave of cold mud, and the gun fell just out of my reach. I looked up, not sure of how bad I'd been hit, and there was Bart Gibson.

He was just lowering his handgun. I was scared, but at the same time the fear felt far away. On the surface I was calm.

"If there's any hope for a renegade to be saved, Lord," I prayed, "don't let him kill me until I am."

But I thought like as not that my time had come. I was going to find out the long and the short of it soon, I reckoned.

"Hullo, Gibson," I said, and my voice, though it come out husky, was cheerful.

"I'm mighty glad you got religion, boy; you're about ready to cash in on it," he said.

"Well go ahead."

He shook his head. "Not yet. I want to know something. And how fast you tell me's gonna have a lot to do with the way I put you out of your misery."

I felt bad about having lied to the good folk about things, but I wasn't yet repentant enough to feel bad about lying to Gibson. "You're chasing a dream, Gibson," I told him. "There ain't no money."

"Josiah junior," he said, and he eased back the hammer of the gun. "I know there's money."

The rain suddenly slacked up some, and I could see him better.

"I know," he said. "Because that lying, drunk, dirty father of yours won twenty thousand dollars from me at poker the week before I visited him."

"So that's it," I said. "Pa was mighty good at poker, all right."

"He cheated."

"He cheated greenhorns, Gibson. He never risked cheating a man who knew the game."

Gibson pointed the gun down at me. "Where is it?"

"In the hills, Gibson—but if he cheated you, why didn't you just call him on it? Wasn't there witnesses?" I asked. It was hard to talk because my leg was hurting like fire, and the mud was chilling me through.

"We played with four of us at the table," Gibson said. "But the other two went on their way. They were cattle investors."

I coughed out a laugh. "He got you all right, with your wallet full from a cattle sale."

"Shut up!" He let the gun go off, and a bullet flew past my ear.

"You know he didn't cheat you," I gasped. "You know it, Gibson. That's why you couldn't call him on it. He'd have called back those witnesses and proved it."

"I got you in the leg, boy, and the right shoulder's next," he said. "Unless you tell me where it is."

"Put down that gun!"

Gibson froze, and just his eyes looked up. I knew that voice. It was Sister Harford.

I craned my head around as best I could and got a glimpse of her standing in the street with a rifle at her shoulder. Gibson lowered the gun but didn't drop it.

"Ornery," I whispered.

"Listen here, spinster lady," he called to her. "You get off the street, you hear me?"

"I promise you, Mr. Gibson, if you do not drop that gun, I shall shoot you down."

"Gibson," I said in a low voice. "Don't hurt her. I'll tell you where the money is—it's in the higher cave where your men trailed me. There's a stump of candle fixed by the wall, and the money's hid in the rocks only five paces away."

He gave no sign of hearing me. "You gonna risk getting shot for some renegade's kid?" he demanded. "I'd as soon shoot him as spit on him."

"If you raise that gun, I'll shoot you myself," she promised. "Drop the gun."

He suddenly whirled the gun up, not at me, but at her, and I screamed, "No!" and strained to get the gun I'd dropped, but before he fired off a shot, another rifle went off from one of the alleyways. Gibson dropped like a stone into the mud. Sister Harford, without another thought for whoever was back there, ran to me.

Curly Rush came running from cover, calling out to us that it was just him and not to be afraid. He ran up to Gibson's body and knelt by it in the mud.

"Curly!" I exclaimed.

"He's dead, Josiah. But he'd have kilt the spinster. I had to do it." All the same, Curly stood up and burst out crying. He'd never been a fighting man, and I knew he was thinking of Mrs. Gibson and the girls. I felt mighty bad too. I'd never wanted it to come to this.

Chapter 26

True Religion

The town settled down. After Gibson's fall, there was no more talk of lynching and no more talk of money. It was like everybody wanted to forget everything that had happened. If I wasn't as welcome as I had been, at least I wasn't in danger anymore.

I spent a good deal of time with Getty Coleman. He visited me often up in my room at Sister Harford's while I recovered from the leg wound. I told him about what I'd prayed when Gibson had dropped me in the street.

"Only," I added, "I didn't mean that God should kill Gibson."

"God gives every man his number of days, Josiah," Getty Coleman told me. "Believe me, if Gibson had been concerned about his soul, time would have been made for him. But all he cared about was that money."

Then we got quiet, until at last Coleman said, "Well, you asked for time, Josiah, and God gave you time. Do you understand what I told you that day?"

"I think I understand it better," I said. "I was trying hard to be good and to fit in. But that's not the same as what you have."

"No, it's not." Coleman said. "In fact, the Bible tells us that we go with Jesus outside the camp, bearing His reproach. That means that sometimes Christians can never fit in. Like when it comes to lynching, maybe, or standing by while a young boy is murdered. Christianity means belonging to Jesus and having Him work in you to change your nature to be like His."

"So getting saved means . . ."

"Repenting. And trusting," Coleman said.

"I understand now." And I did. I knew, after everything God had done for me, that there had to be mercy for me. So at last I gave up on getting religion and got saved. Coleman was so natural about talking about the Lord that I didn't feel odd praying in front of him. I'd prayed so many false prayers that I wasn't perfectly sure how to say what I sincerely wanted to say, and now I don't recall the exact prayer, but I remember how new and wonderful it was to me that Christ came to save sinners. I felt as though He'd come just for me and had given me Getty Coleman and Sister Harford all for myself—like they were the signs of His good will toward me. It was easy to believe that He could have mercy on me when I considered how He'd brought me out of so much trouble.

And speaking of the troubles the Lord had brought me out of, there was the money to think of. That was my first concern after I got saved. I wondered if I should give the twenty thousand dollars to Mrs. Gibson, but Coleman didn't think it would be wise.

"They're selling out and going East," he told me. "They don't need the money, if that's what you're worried about, and they won't want to hear your story. I don't think they knew that their husband and father lost that much in a poker game with a renegade. They wouldn't believe you, and they wouldn't want the money, Josiah."

"I don't want it," I said. "It's got blood all over it, Brother Coleman. It's been a curse to every man who's ever had it."

"Powerful lot of good can be done with that money," he observed.

"Maybe so, but all it's done is a powerful lot of harm. Still," I added, "if you'll promise never to mention it to me again, I'll draw you a map that will show you where to find it. You can give it away. Just don't ever tell me about it."

He shook his head. "You're young yet. You ought to decide on it when you're older."

Coleman had already arranged for his men to go out and fence in Pa's old claim again. As soon as I was able, I was going to go out to Coleman's place and help him on his spread. In turn he'd help me and get me started again in cattle. Anybody doing that much for me deserved the money, I reckoned, but Coleman didn't want it for himself.

"I don't know how to rightly thank you for all you've done," I said to him. We heard Sister Harford coming up the steps just then.

"Well, actually, boy, I guess I'm the one that's in your debt," he said as she came in with a tray of tea for us. He took it from her and set it on the stand by the bed. But there was something in the way he did it that made me think that something had changed.

"Take the chair," he told her.

"No, you sit. You two look like conspirators," she said, and as he sat down she dropped her hands on his shoulder. I looked from her to him. She looked prim a second and then smiled, and he laughed out loud.

"I'm always gonna get you to do my speaking for me, boy!" he exclaimed. "You see, things have changed somewhat since we laid you down up here to mend."

"You said yes at last?" I asked her. She colored pink again, but he and she looked at each other real happy.

"I realized that he'd never find another woman worthy of him," she said with some spirit.

He laughed again. "Don't never need to look, neither, after this June. Come summer you'll be spending many a cozy evening with us out on the ranch, Josiah!"

Epilogue

Brother Coleman and Sister Harford got married that June. And just like they promised, we spent many a cozy evening together out at the ranch.

As for the money, I was some troubled by it, knowing that a big pile of money can do a big pile of good. So I fretted and stewed some months until the next thaw. The spring floods caused a powerful big avalanche up on the mountains, and the higher cave was partly filled in. That money couldn't be dug out in a hundred years.

So there it lies. The cattle do well down on my small ranch, and I'm bringing in some short horns. The shanty is up, and I'm adding to it this summer.